**"No." Again Joe answered
on behalf of his daughter.**

Felicity drew in a deep breath. She spoke calmly. "I think Samantha might be better qualified to answer that question than you, Dr. Petersen."

The muscular twitch in the man's face gave away the incredulity his tone managed to conceal. "I believe my daughter has a greenstick fracture of the left radius. Perhaps you could do whatever baseline measurements your protocols dictate and then find a doctor who can authorize the necessary pain relief and treatment this injury requires."

Felicity met his stare with equal directness. "I *am* a doctor, as a matter of fact. I'm one of the consultants in the emergency department." She allowed only a moment to let the implications sink in before adding a punch line she couldn't quite resist. "And don't worry, Dr. Petersen. I may not be a neurosurgeon but I *do* know what I'm doing."

Dear Reader,

Perhaps you are driving home one evening, when you spot a rotating flashing light or hear a siren. Instantly, your pulse quickens—it's human nature. You can't help responding to these signals that there is an emergency somewhere close by.

HEARTBEAT, romances being published in North America for the first time, brings you the fast-paced kinds of stories that trigger responses to life-and-death situations. The heroes and heroines, whose lives you will share in this exciting series of books, devote themselves to helping others, to saving lives, to *caring*. And while they are devotedly doing what they do best, they manage to fall in love!

Since these books are largely set in the U.K., Australia and New Zealand, and mainly written by authors who reside in those countries, the medical terms originally used may be unfamiliar to North American readers. Because we wanted to ensure that you enjoyed these stories as thoroughly as possible, we've taken a few special measures. Within the stories themselves, we have substituted American terms for British ones we felt would be very unfamiliar to you. And we've also included in these books a short glossary of terms that we've left in the stories, so as not to disturb their authenticity, but that you might wonder about.

So prepare to feel your heart beat a little faster! You're about to experience love when life is on the line!

Yours sincerely,

Marsha Zinberg,
Executive Editor, Harlequin Books

DOUBLE DUTY

Alison Roberts

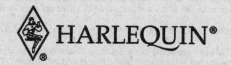

TORONTO • NEW YORK • LONDON
AMSTERDAM • PARIS • SYDNEY • HAMBURG
STOCKHOLM • ATHENS • TOKYO • MILAN • MADRID
PRAGUE • WARSAW • BUDAPEST • AUCKLAND

ISBN 0-373-51258-9

DOUBLE DUTY

First North American Publication 2003

Alison Roberts lives in Christchurch, New Zealand. She began her working career as a primary school teacher but now splits her available working hours between writing and active duty as an ambulance officer. Throwing in a large dose of parenting, housework, gardening and pet minding keeps life busy, and teenage daughter Becky is responsible for an increasing number of days spent on equestrian pursuits. Finding time for everything can be a challenge but the rewards make the effort more than worthwhile.

GLOSSARY

A and E—accident and emergency department

B and G—bloods and glucose

Consultant—an experienced specialist registrar who is the leader of a medical team; there can be a junior and senior consultant on a team

CVA—cerebrovascular accident

Duty registrar—the doctor on call

FBC—full blood count

Fixator—an external device, a kind of frame, for rigidly holding bones together while they heal

GA—general anesthetic

GCS—the Glasgow Coma Scale, used to determine a patient's level of consciousness

Houseman/house officer—British equivalent of a medical intern or clerk

MI—myocardial infarction

Obs—observations re: pulse, blood pressure, etc.

Registrar/specialist registrar—a doctor who is trained in a particular area of medicine

Resus—room or unit where a patient is taken for resuscitation after cardiac accident

Rostered—scheduled

RTA—road traffic accident

Senior House Officer (SHO)—British equivalent of a resident

Theatre—operating room

CHAPTER ONE

SEVEN-THIRTY a.m.

Far too early to be starting work. A job like this might be OK in summer but below zero temperatures weren't much fun. Not when the first rays of sunshine only made up for their lack of warmth by the uncomfortably blinding glare they could produce. Jeff Simms shaded his eyes from the glare with his hand. He could see the group of men congregating around the prefabricated shed that served as headquarters for the building site. He could also see his mate, Lou, climbing out of Tommo's truck just ahead of him.

At least they'd made it to work on time today. The boss should be looking a lot happier than he appeared to be. Maybe he hadn't had his coffee yet. The thought of coffee was enticing. Jeff and Lou had downed quite a few beers during their session at the pub last night.

'Hey!'

'How's it going, mate?' Jeff grinned at Lou.

'Have you spoken to the boss yet?'

'No. I just got here. Bloody cold, eh?' Jeff blew

on his knuckles and rubbed his hands together vigorously.

'Tommo reckons you're in trouble, mate.'

'What for?' Jeff caught Lou's eye. Maybe they shouldn't have taken off to the pub yesterday with such alacrity.

'Boss couldn't find his skill saw last night,' Tommo reported gloomily. 'He reckons you'd been using it.'

'I was,' Jeff admitted. 'I had to go up and tidy that framing on the second floor.'

'Where'd you put the saw, then?'

Jeff's gaze roamed the scaffolding on the apartment block. He traced the route on the corner that he'd used to climb down from the wooden planks, trying to remember just what he had been carrying. The oath that escaped his lips was enough to impress even Tommo.

'It's still up there.'

Tommo unleashed an even better oath. 'It'll be frozen solid. Man, are you in trouble!'

'It'll still be dry. I put it under a tarpaulin. That's why I forgot about it. I'll go and get it now.'

'You can't.' Lou shook his head. 'Scaffolding's out of bounds until it thaws. The boss'll go mental if he sees you.'

'He won't see me. It's on the road side. I'll be quick.'

'You'd better be careful, mate.' Lou sounded doubtful. 'It's solid ice up there.'

Seven thirty-five a.m.

It was just as well he'd set off this early. Joe Petersen drummed his fingers on the steering-wheel as he waited in the line of traffic for the lights to change. He needed to get right across town and it was going to take a long time at this rate. He'd promised to be there at 8 a.m. to help get the kids off to school and then take Samantha to kindergarten for the morning. Dayna wouldn't be very impressed if he arrived late, and he wasn't about to give her any new ammunition regarding his lack of elementary parenting skills.

Joe glanced sideways to give his eyes a rest from the glare of the rising sun. The building site to his left was impressively large. This part of Christchurch city had changed beyond recognition since he'd last driven past but that was hardly surprising. It had been nearly five years since he'd had a visit lasting more than a few days. The trend seemed to be towards building these large inner-city apartment blocks now and this one looked fairly up-market. Joe's idle gaze roamed the side of the well-formed building. He could see the ice coating the scaffolding. Cold job, being a builder at this time of year. He wondered idly what the young chap was doing, scrambling up the side of the steel skeleton. He seemed to be in rather a hurry.

The toot from behind indicated that Joe's attention should be back on the traffic. He slid the car back into gear but the movement he caught in his peripheral vision jerked his gaze back to the left. Had the lad's foot slipped on that wooden platform? He'd managed to catch hold of one of the steel pipes but the grip held only momentarily. Joe watched the fall with horror. He could almost feel the impact as the victim's back contacted the next steel bar several feet below before the graceful arc that completed the fall.

The sensation of horror was dismissed instantly and replaced with a clinical detachment. The impact mid-fall had been enough to cause a lumbar spinal injury. The distraction to the cervical vertebrae which the impact of landing on his head might have caused was even more serious. Joe pulled his steering-wheel decisively and put his foot down on the accelerator to gain just enough momentum for the wheels to mount the curb. He pushed the hazard light control on the dashboard.

Seven thirty-eight a.m.

Felicity Munroe shaded her eyes from the glare of the sun. It was hard to see what was going on ahead but the traffic appeared to be even slower than normal for this time of day. At least she wasn't too far from the hospital now. With a bit of luck she could still make the 8 a.m. meeting with members of the cardiology department. The interface between Cardiology and Emergency needed some urgent attention. Only yesterday they'd had a patient with a major heart attack taking an unacceptable length of time to clear the emergency department.

Her scrutiny revealed the cause of the hold-up. A car had pulled off the road onto the footpath but was still creating enough of an obstacle to cause problems. The vehicle's hazard lights were flashing and a man was attempting to get out on the driver's side. Passing traffic was making this difficult, however, and the man was being subjected to irate blasts of car horns as he tried to open his door.

Traffic ground to a complete halt again with one car close enough to provide an impassable barrier to the man in the stalled vehicle. Felicity could see him moving to exit from the passenger side with some urgency. Her own car was still well away from the disruption, level with the entrance to a building site on her left. Felicity glanced sideways briefly, hoping to distract herself from a mounting irritation with the delay. She'd been watching the huge apartment block take shape for months now and the site looked busy again this morning. Extraordinarily busy, in fact. There were people running from all directions.

Felicity's casual glance focused on the scene sharply. On the supine figure that the men were running towards.

The wisdom gleaned from years of experience was not needed to let Felicity know that a significant incident had occurred. It took only a second to ease her vehicle from the line of traffic and cruise onto the building site. A few seconds more and she was at the side of the victim. She could see that the young man was conscious and breathing. She picked up his wrist to check the radial pulse as she crouched down beside him.

'Can anyone tell me what's happened?'

'Don't touch that man! Stand back!'

The command was vehement enough to distract Felicity from her visual examination of her patient. The sharp tone made the man crouching beside her stand up hurriedly, stunning him into silence, though he had barely begun to answer Felicity's query.

'I'm sure you all have the best intentions,' the man told the group. 'But people who don't know what they're doing can actually do more harm than good in a situation like this. I'm a doctor,' he continued. 'And I witnessed the accident.' He glared at Felicity, his gaze flicking over her well-dressed slight figure dismissively. 'You haven't tried to *move* him, have you?'

'Of course not.' Felicity might not have witnessed

the accident at first hand but it didn't take much common sense to realise that someone lying motionless beneath scaffolding could well have suffered a significant fall. And it didn't take anything like her training to suggest that such a fall carried a high index of suspicion of a spinal injury. Felicity opened her mouth to inform this man that as an emergency department consultant she was hardly likely to risk an exacerbation of such an injury by moving an unstabilised patient. She was also tempted to say something snappy regarding the assumptions this man had clearly made based on what she looked like. What did he think she did for a job? Work as a beauty therapist perhaps? Not that she was given a chance to say anything at all.

'Move over here.' The stranger draped the stethoscope he was holding around his neck with a casual movement that suggested long familiarity. 'You can do something useful and hold this chap's head still. It's very important that he doesn't move his neck.'

Felicity surprised herself by doing as she was asked. Or, rather, told. There was something about this man's attitude that indicated it wouldn't be in anyone's best interests to get in his way right now and it certainly wasn't an appropriate time to voice her resentment at the way he was treating her. Felicity took a mental step backwards. She would only intervene if she needed to and so far she had no complaints.

The doctor had gently moved the young man's head and neck into a neutral position. As soon as Felicity's hands took over providing support he conducted a rapid examination of the head and neck. Felicity relaxed a little as she noted that his movements appeared to indicate that he knew what he was doing. From the gentle palpation of the front of the neck he was clearly checking for tracheal deviation. As he carefully felt the back of the victim's neck, the young man groaned and Felicity watched the doctor's face register a focused concern.

'I need some sandbags,' he stated. 'Or cushions. Or some rolled-up clothing. Anything. We need to pad the neck to protect it. And someone call an ambulance.' He leaned over his patient, seemingly oblivious to how close this brought his face to Felicity's. 'What's your name?' he queried briskly.

'Jeff.'

'I'm Joe. Joe Petersen. I'm a neurosurgeon.'

Felicity blinked. Perhaps the stranger *was* more qualified to deal with a spinal injury than she was. The fact that she'd never heard the name associated with the specialised spinal injuries unit on the other side of town didn't mean he wasn't an expert. He could be visiting from overseas. His deep voice did have the hint of an unusual accent.

'I can't feel my legs.' Jeff's words held an edge of panic. 'Am I going to be paralysed?'

'Are you having any trouble breathing?'

'No.'

Felicity tightened her grip at the attempt to shake his head. 'Keep very still, Jeff,' she told him. 'It's important.'

'He hasn't told me.' Jeff caught Felicity's gaze. 'I want to know how bad this is.'

'We don't know yet.' Joe placed the earpieces of his stethoscope into position. He pulled up the thick jersey Jeff was wearing. 'I'm just going to listen to your chest.'

Felicity could feel the slower than normal heart rate under her fingertips. She considered suggesting that neurogenic shock could be producing a brady-cardia as she watched Joe conduct a rapid assess-ment of Jeff's chest, abdomen and pelvic area. He pressed his hands on each side of Jeff's hips to check the stability of the pelvis. Glancing up, he noticed Felicity's studied gaze.

'I'm looking for what we call "silent" lesions,' he informed her. 'Injuries, that is.'

Felicity kept her face neutral. She was perfectly well aware what lesions were. It was quite interest-ing, being treated as a layperson. Or it would have been if this man's tone didn't suggest that her level of intelligence might not be up to scratch. She decided not to raise the subject of neurogenic shock.

'If there's a significant level of paralysis then injuries could be hidden.' Joe was palpating Jeff's abdomen with obvious skill. 'That means they won't be causing any pain. I'm particularly concerned with a chest injury that might affect breathing or something that could cause internal bleeding. Can you feel me touching you, Jeff?'

'No, I can't feel anything. Have I broken my back?'

'You've certainly injured your spine.' The assessment for major associated injuries had taken less than a minute. Joe moved swiftly into a neurological check that Felicity could also make no complaints about.

'Can you move your hands, Jeff?'

'I think so.' Jeff's fingers wiggled weakly. 'They feel weird, though.'

'What sort of weird?'

'Kind of pins and needles.'

'Can you feel me touching them?' Joe went from a light touch to a distinct pinch before Jeff responded.

'Kind of.'

'Which finger am I touching?' Joe was pinching Jeff's thumb.

'I'm not sure. The middle one?'

Felicity saw the frown of concentration as Joe assimilated the information of lowered sensation. He took hold of Jeff's hands. 'Squeeze my hands,' he ordered. 'As hard as you can.'

The pulses on both wrists were checked and then Joe moved to check Jeff's legs. As he elicited the assistance of Jeff's friend, Lou, to remove the laces of the steel-capped boots and ease the heavy footwear clear, Felicity found she was still focused on Joe Petersen's face. It was a very intelligent face with rugged features and dark brown eyes that seemed almost grim in their intensity. Straight brown hair revealed distinct auburn tints as the early morning sunshine bathed the group of people. What a strange thing to notice at a time like this, Felicity thought. She transferred her gaze to the knot of anxious-faced men surrounding them. They were still standing well back, except for one younger man who pushed through the group.

'I've found some sandbags.'

'Good for you, Tommo.' The men made way for him.

'Excellent,' Joe added. 'Well done.' Felicity noticed the pleased expression on the young man's face as Joe rose swiftly from his crouched position. Joe clearly had the ability to lead people. Tommo's face became eager.

'Where would you like me to put the bags?'

'Give them to me,' Joe ordered. 'I need to put them in exactly the right place.'

Felicity saw the disappointment that accompanied the handover of the sandbags. Joe Petersen might have leadership qualities but he would never hold the loyalty of the people he led if he dismissed their potential so abruptly. There wasn't anything highly technical about the placement of support materials for a neck and head. Tommo could easily have been directed to accomplish the task. He would have had the satisfaction of knowing he was really helping and Joe would have had a loyal assistant for anything else he might require. The sandbags were cold against Felicity's hands as Joe snuggled them along the side of Jeff's head.

'Don't let go of his head,' Joe instructed her firmly. 'These supports will help but they're not enough. You're doing a great job,' he added.

It was the first direct eye contact Felicity had had with this man. It was also the first appreciative comment. She noted that the dark brown eyes were rather attractive but she couldn't detect any hint of personal warmth being directed at her. In fact, in the few minutes so far of his management of this incident, Felicity had not seen even a hint of a smile. Joe was focused on this task with an intensity that was definitely grim. The people around him were merely tools. His praise of Felicity's ability to stabilise his patient's head and his appreciation of Tommo's success in locating sandbags was automatic, an acknowledgment that they had both performed as he had expected. How totally ridiculous that she should feel as pleased by the acknowledgement as Tommo had been.

Felicity gave herself a mental shake. She could hear the wail of the approaching siren advertising the imminent arrival of the ambulance service. The emergency vehicle was likely to be crewed by paramedics who would know who she was. It was going to be extremely interesting to see how Joe reacted to finding out her qualifications. Felicity was also curious to observe how he would relate to the ambulance officers. Doctors who had no direct contact with the service were sometimes inclined towards an arrogant assumption that the paramedics were no more than drivers. Given Joe's treatment of the people around him so far, Felicity would be surprised if he gave the paramedics any credit for the skills she knew they possessed.

The first surprise came when Joe stood up to greet Stanley Ferris, the paramedic leading the crew.

'I'm Joe Petersen. I'm a neurosurgeon,' Joe told Stanley crisply. 'This is Jeff. He's nineteen years old and has fallen approximately fifteen metres from this scaffolding.'

Stanley glanced up at the platform well above them as he took in the mechanism of injury.

'He hit a rail about halfway down which caught his back in the lumbar region. Then he landed on his head, causing a distraction injury to his neck. He wasn't KO'd and his GCS has remained at 15.' Joe cast a brief glance at the second ambulance officer. 'Can you get a cervical collar on Jeff? Thanks. And some oxygen. A high-concentration mask.' His attention turned back to Stanley.

'Jeff has pain at C5 to C7 and I'd query an increased interspinous gap. He has a moderate contusion in the occipital area. He has paralysis to both legs and paraesthesia and paresis in both arms and hands. Chest and abdomen are clear, breathing is diaphragmatic. He's bradycardic at 55 and I'm concerned about hypothermia. This ground is frozen solid and it's been nearly ten minutes since the accident.'

Felicity watched as Stanley nodded to show he had absorbed the information. She was impressed at Joe's professional summary of their patient's condition, but she was even more impressed at his attitude towards Stanley. Assuming he now had assistance of medical merit, Joe was treating the paramedic as a colleague and an intelligent one at that.

'We need some blankets,' Joe continued. 'A foil

sheet if you have one. Jeff will be poikilothermic with a spinal injury.'

Felicity's raised eyebrow mirrored Stanley's expression. Perhaps Joe wasn't treating Stanley as a colleague after all. Did the paramedic know that poikilothermic meant that a body would assume the temperature of the environment? Maybe Joe was deliberately using terms even medical staff might not recognise easily in order to show superiority and demonstrate his command of the situation.

'We need to get him off the ground as quickly as possible,' Joe continued. 'Do you carry backboards or scoop stretchers?'

'Both.' Stanley's glance at Jeff's position made him notice Felicity for the first time. His eyes widened dramatically. Felicity's smile was intended to indicate that this wasn't the moment for Stanley to be distracted by her presence, and the paramedic took the hint with his customary astuteness. 'A scoop stretcher will let us pick him up with minimal disruption but they are cold. If we log-roll him onto a backboard it would also give you the chance to check his lower back.'

'What's going to be quicker?'

'Probably the scoop.'

'We'll do that, then.' Joe watched as Stanley and his partner, Ray, introduced themselves to Jeff and explained what they were about to do. They moved the sandbags and eased a cervical collar into place.

'Grab a towel,' Stanley directed Ray. 'We want that under his head to maintain neutral alignment. You can get the scoop out as well. I'll take some vitals while you set it up.'

Stanley wrapped a blood-pressure cuff around Jeff's arm. Ray brought the metal scoop stretcher from the back of the ambulance. When Joe moved to take over unfolding and setting out the stretcher, Stanley caught Felicity's gaze.

'Does he have any idea who you are?'

'No.' Felicity couldn't help a quick grin. 'I haven't exactly had the opportunity to introduce myself.'

'Hmm.' Stanley's noncommittal grunt acknowledged the level of authority Joe had assumed. 'At least he seems to know what he's talking about.'

Felicity nodded. She rubbed her hands together. They were cold and stiff after the long minutes of stabilising Jeff's head and neck. 'I think I'll leave you guys to it,' she told Stanley. 'I'm late for a meeting and I'm sure Mr Petersen can give you any medical assistance you need.'

Stanley was taking some intravenous supplies from his kit. He had the line in Jeff's hand within seconds. Joe frowned as he noticed the action that had been taken without his direction. He laid down the half of the scoop stretcher he was carrying.

'Blood pressure's 85 over 60,' Stanley told him. 'I won't run any IV fluids unless the systolic drops below 80.'

Joe nodded and Felicity could sense his satisfaction. The low blood pressure with a spinal injury was likely to be due to vasodilation below the level of injury rather than blood loss. As long as the systolic blood pressure remained above renal filtration pressure of 80 mm mercury it was not advisable to give extra IV fluids, which could cause complications from over-hydration.

Joe was eyeing the drug supplies in Stanley's kit. 'Are you able to give a loading dose of methyl prednisolone?'

'No.' Stanley shook his head. 'That's not in our procedures.'

'We do it in some parts of the States.' Joe frowned again. 'Have you got a specialist spinal unit we can transfer him to directly?'

'We go through the emergency department at the main hospital. It's only five minutes away. They'll stabilise him and then transfer. It takes nearly an hour for a slow transport of an acute case to the spinal unit.' Stanley's glance at Felicity suggested that it was time she introduced herself but Felicity was quite happy with the management of their patient.

'I'd better go,' she announced. 'Unless I can help in some other way?'

'No, of course not.' Joe looked vaguely surprised at the offer. 'We've got plenty of extra hands here. Thanks for your help.'

'My pleasure.' Felicity threw a glance over her shoulder as she walked back towards her car. The blades of the scoop stretcher had been eased, one side at a time, beneath Jeff. The halves had been clicked into place and Jeff was now being strapped into position. The scene had been well managed and any injury Jeff had sustained had been in no way exacerbated. No doubt she would see the young fall victim later on in the emergency department. He would probably still be accompanied by the neurosurgeon, who seemed determined to take complete control of his management.

Felicity shook her head as she joined the line of traffic again. Maybe she should have asserted herself and let him know that she wasn't simply a useful pair of extra hands. It had been a little immature to take offence at the suggestion that she didn't know what she was doing. It wasn't as if he could have had any idea she was remotely qualified to act as a colleague, but his attitude had rankled. She had worked long and hard to get where she was now.

His dismissal of her, based presumably on what she looked like, had got right up her nose. She was regretting the decision to stay anonymous now, however. It would have been more interesting to have had a professional discussion. She'd like to know where in the States they were doing methyl prednisolone protocols in the field and whether it had been going on long enough to have results on any improvement in long-term outcome. The lights changed and Felicity moved off with a sigh. It was too late now. Best she forget about the whole encounter.

The intention to forget wasn't easily acted upon. The encounter had left an impression that lasted well past the meeting with the cardiology department. It was still ready to jump into prominence later that morning when Felicity noticed Stanley and Ray handing over another patient to the sorting nurse. She waited until they had transferred their patient to a bed.

'You guys did a good job with that spinal patient this morning.'

'Thanks,' Stanley responded warmly. 'It was a surprise to see you there, Fliss.'

'I was just passing. I became rapidly redundant.' Felicity's smile gave no hint of her persistent dissatisfaction with the incident. 'How did the transport go? Did Mr Petersen go with you?'

'No, thank goodness.' Stanley grinned. 'He probably would have complained about every bump on the road. He was a bit over the top, wasn't he?'

'He knew what he was doing. I think he was just determined to manage things as well as possible.' Felicity was surprised to find herself defending Joe, but it would have been unprofessional to complain about another doctor to Stanley despite their long association and Felicity's appreciation of the paramedic's level of skill. 'Jeff was lucky to have someone that experienced on the scene. I imagine that Mr Petersen is only visiting. It sounded as though he's come from the States.'

'He's been in the States but he's just moved back to New Zealand.' Stanley fished in his pocket and extracted a slip of paper. 'He gave me his phone number. He said he'd like to hear some follow-up if I had the chance.'

'Oh.' Felicity dismissed the errant thought that she could do the follow-up and contact Joe herself. Why on earth would she want to do that?

'He's looking for a job,' Stanley told her. 'We had a quick chat while he was giving me his number. Apparently he's just finished some postgraduate specialist training and he's come back here for family reasons. He's hoping to get a position here or at the spinal unit.'

'Unusual to move countries without a position to

go to,' Felicity observed. 'Rather a big risk, especially for a consultant. Did he say what the family reasons were?'

'No. But they must have been compelling. He was dead keen to get away as soon as we'd loaded Jeff. Said he didn't want to let his daughter down.' Stanley's pager sounded at the same instant that Felicity's beeper went off. They both grinned.

'No rest for the wicked. See you later, Fliss.'

'No doubt. Bye, Stan.' Felicity moved towards the telephone on the sorting desk. This morning's incident had simply been an interesting and somewhat different start to the day. Now it was time to get on with the many and varied challenges the emergency department could throw at her. She was bound to see Stan again in the near future. She was not likely, however, to see Joe Petersen again, and that was fine. It might have been satisfying to tell him who she was, but if she'd wanted to see him again she could have offered to take that phone number from Stan and use the excuse of a patient follow-up as a reason for contact. The choice had been there and it hadn't been difficult to make. She had no desire to renew her acquaintance with Joe Petersen. The incident and the man were history.

In fact, she would probably have trouble recognising him if she *did* see him again.

CHAPTER TWO

THE recognition was instantaneous.

Felicity spotted Joe in the emergency department from as far away as it was possible to get. She was entering the double doors that led from the end of the corridor dividing the department into the main area of Queen Mary Hospital. Joe was standing beside the bed in cubicle 3. On top of the bed sat a small girl with curly red hair. Even from that distance Felicity could recognise a struggle to keep on top of the fear, confusion and probably pain the child was experiencing.

The characteristic decisiveness in Felicity's forward movement took her swiftly towards the sorting desk.

'Who's in cubicle 3, Mike?'

The nurse manager had been talking to senior consultant Gareth Harvey as he was entering information into a computer program. 'Samantha Petersen. Four years old. Query greenstick fracture of the left radius.'

Felicity nodded. Joe Petersen's daughter, then. Part of the family whose circumstances had somehow brought Joe to Christchurch. 'Did she come in by ambulance?'

'No. Her father brought her in a couple of minutes ago. He's some sort of medic, apparently.' Mike raised an eyebrow as he glanced up from the computer screen, clearly puzzled by the interest shown by a consultant in such a minor case.

'Do you know him?' Gareth also looked curious.

'We've met.' Felicity's gaze flicked to the whiteboard. The spaces beside cubicle 3 had yet to be filled in.

Mike had followed her line of query. 'I'm giving her to Mary. Colin White can see her later.'

Felicity's gaze shifted again. The nurse, Mary, was pushing an IV trolley out of cubicle 6 so she hadn't caught up on her new case assignment. She knew that Colin, one of the registrars, was still busy in the observation ward she had just come from herself. Nobody had attended to the Petersens yet.

'I'll deal with it, Mike. I've got a clear space unless there's something urgent on the way.'

'Nothing major. Possible infarction coming from out of town but they're twenty minutes or so away yet.'

'OK.' Felicity's nod was brisk. 'This shouldn't take long.' She was already moving towards cubicle 3. It might not take very long but, boy, was she going to enjoy it! She pulled the curtain closed around the cubicle to create a more private examination area.

'Hi, there, sweetheart.' Felicity smiled at the child whose right arm was clutching a soft toy that looked like some kind of floppy dog. 'What's your name?'

Small lips pressed together tightly but the movement was not enough to stop a noticeable chin wobble. Large, frightened brown eyes were fixed on Felicity.

'Tell the nurse your name, Samantha.' The order was given in a kindly voice but the only effect was to make the child's eyes swim with tears.

Felicity flicked Joe a brief glance. *Nurse* indeed. This was going to be even better than she had anticipated. She smiled at Joe's daughter again.

'My name's Fliss,' she told the child. 'Do you go to school, Samantha?'

'She's not old enough for school. She goes to kindergarten.' Joe's tone was wary. Felicity knew he had recognised her now. His brain was ticking over, probably remembering their encounter with the spinal injury patient. Maybe he was wondering if he might have insulted her by not knowing she was a nurse. Nurse, ha! Felicity bit back a tiny smile. Joe would keep for the moment.

'Do they call you Samantha at kindy, sweetheart?'

This time Felicity was rewarded with an almost imperceptible head shake.

'What do they call you? Sam? Sammie?'

The slight movement changed to an affirmative direction. Felicity mirrored the nod as she perched casually on the bed beside the small girl.

'Which do you like better? Sam or Sammie?'

'Sam.' The response was a whisper.

Felicity lowered her own voice to a similarly conspiratorial level. 'Can I call you Sam?'

'OK.'

'Cool.' Felicity winked at Samantha. 'I'll call you Sam and you can call me Fliss. Is that a deal?'

The smile was worth winning. It brightened up a pale little face which was dusted with freckles that matched the luxurious reddish blonde curls. Felicity's visual impression had included more than the skin colour of her patient, however. She had, by now, assessed the level of the child's responsiveness and distress, noted her respiration rate and seen the slight but obvious deformity of the left forearm that lay limply on the child's lap. The right arm still clutched the tattered toy dog.

'How did you hurt your arm, Sam?'

'I...I fell out of the swing.' The child's glance towards her father made Felicity blink. Was Samantha afraid of giving the wrong answer? Was she afraid of her *father*? The continuation of the hesitant response raised Felicity's suspicions another notch.

'I…I didn't hang on tight enough.' A huge tear escaped and rolled down a freckled cheek.

'It was an accident.' Was Joe Petersen annoyed with the child or the inconvenience of a trip to the emergency department? Whatever the reason, the tone was inappropriate and not the normal interaction between a parent and child in such a situation. Felicity had already noted the lack of physical contact between the pair. What was going on here?

'It doesn't matter how it happened,' she told Samantha gently. 'What matters is that we fix up your arm. Does it hurt at the moment?'

Samantha nodded.

'Did you hit your head when you fell out of the swing?'

'She wasn't KO'd,' Joe said.

Felicity ignored him. 'Does anything else hurt you, Sam?'

'No.' Again Joe answered on behalf of his daughter.

Felicity drew in a deep breath. She spoke calmly. 'I think Samantha might be better qualified to answer that question than you, Mr Petersen.'

The muscular twitch in the man's face gave away the incredulity his tone managed to conceal. 'I believe my daughter has a greenstick fracture of the left radius. Perhaps you could do whatever baseline measurements your protocols dictate and then find a doctor who can authorise the necessary pain relief and treatment this injury requires.'

Felicity met the stare with equal directness. 'I *am* a doctor, as a matter of fact. I'm one of the consultants in this emergency department.' She allowed only a moment to let the implications sink in before adding a punchline she couldn't quite resist. 'And don't worry, Mr Petersen. I may not be a neurosurgeon but I *do* know what I'm doing.'

She turned back to Samantha, satisfied that the stunned and distinctly discomfited expression on Joe's face would take some time to dissipate.

'I know your arm is sore, sweetheart, but I want you to try and wiggle your fingers for me. Can you do that?'

The movement produced was tentative but reassuring. 'Good girl, Sam. That's fantastic. Now, I'm going to hold your hand—just gently. Can you feel me touching your fingers?' Felicity noted the temperature and colour of Samantha's hand as she responded affirmatively. 'OK, see if you can squeeze my fingers.'

Felicity compared the responses with Samantha's uninjured limb. She could still feel Joe's stare. She checked the radial pulses on both wrists before glancing up. 'No neurological or circulatory deficit. That's good.'

'Why didn't you tell me before?'

'I hadn't done the necessary examination.' Felicity gave in to the temptation to be deliberately obtuse.

'I meant, why didn't you tell me that you were a doctor?'

'I've only been in here a few minutes.'

'I'm not talking about now. I'm talking about last week.' Joe Petersen's tone suggested he was unamused by this verbal sparring.

Felicity shrugged as though it was a matter of little importance. 'I don't remember having the opportunity,' she said thoughtfully. 'You had the situation well controlled—and, anyway,' she added mischievously, 'stabilising the head and neck of a spinal injury patient *is* a pretty useful thing to do.' She turned back to Samantha.

'We're going to get a special picture taken of your arm,' she told the child. 'An X-ray. It looks at the inside of your arm. Do you know what there is inside there?'

Samantha shook her head. The fearful look returned to the large, brown eyes.

'It's nothing to worry about,' Felicity reassured her. 'An X-ray doesn't hurt. It's just a special camera that can see what we can't see. Bones. They're the hard bits inside your arms and legs.' She was debating whether the trauma of inserting an IV line to give some narcotic pain relief was justified, given how easily Samantha could be distracted from her injury. She still looked ready to cry again so Felicity decided to test the distraction level once more.

'Does your dog have a name?'

'Snowy.' The firm response came from Joe.

Felicity saw the expression on Samantha's face and sighed inwardly. The little girl might be distracted from the pain but upsetting her wasn't going to help. Maybe she needed to push a little harder and find out what was going on in this relationship. The vibes she was getting were making her distinctly uneasy now.

'He looks pretty special,' she told Samantha quietly. 'Is his name really Snowy?'

Samantha shook her head slowly and dislodged another tear. Then another. 'His name's not Snowy,' she sobbed. 'His name is Woof Woof Snowball.'

Felicity bit her lip. Her peripheral vision caught the wince on Joe's face and it was extremely hard not to laugh aloud. The neurosurgeon was acutely embarrassed by the childish name for the toy.

'"Woof Woof Snowball",' Felicity repeated with some relish. 'That's a great name.' She peered more closely at the toy. 'He's a rather grubby snowball right now, though. Did he fall out of the swing, too?'

Samantha nodded.

'Did he hurt himself, do you think?'

The head shook this time. The tears were gone

again and Samantha tried to smile. 'I think he just got dirty.'

'Maybe he needs a bath.'

'I'm not allowed to have squashy toys in the bath. Mum says they take too long to dry.'

'Ah.' Felicity digested the information offhand-edly as she began to record her medical observations on Samantha's chart. So there was a mother. Joe's wife, presumably. Maybe there were brothers and sisters as well. A whole family, in fact, including some cute, fluffy dog. 'Have you got a real dog at home, too, Sam?'

'No. Mum doesn't like dogs.'

'Oh.' Felicity continued her rapid note-taking. 'Does Daddy like dogs?'

'I don't know.'

Felicity's glance was too automatic and too quick to hide her astonishment. How could Samantha not know whether her father liked dogs? Joe was frown-ing.

'Of course I like dogs, Sam.'

Felicity tried to dismiss the notions that flitted through her head as she charted some oral analgesics for Samantha and filled in a requisition form for an X-ray. She needed a bit of time to think about this one. Standing up, she smiled brightly at Samantha.

'I like dogs, too,' she told her. 'In fact, I've got a real dog. He's an Irish setter called Rusty.' Her smile widened. 'Maybe I should have called him "Woof Woof Rusty".'

Samantha giggled. It was a delightful chortle that prompted Felicity to reach out and gently ruffle the child's curls. 'Rusty is a lovely dark auburn colour,' she continued. 'But he has long hair on his tail which is much lighter. On the ends it's exactly the same colour as your hair.'

Samantha looked delighted with the information. 'Sometimes Daddy calls me Nas—Nas...' She struggled with the word. 'Nastagmus,' she managed triumphantly. 'He says that's what my hair reminds *him* of.'

'Really?' A nystagmus was a word used to refer to an abnormal and rapid type of involuntary eye movement. She caught Joe's gaze and a lopsided smile appeared on his face.

'She means "nasturtium".'

'Oh!' Felicity grinned. She loved the amusing verbal errors children often made, though she was usually careful not to show her amusement in front of them. It was difficult to hide her delight at present, however, and Felicity knew quite well that Samantha's mistake had only provided part of the pleasure she was experiencing.

That lopsided twist of his lips was the first time she had seen anything like a smile on Joe's face, and its effect was dramatic. His features softened and crinkles appeared around his eyes. The dark brown eyes were exactly the same colour as Samantha's. In fact, Samantha looked very much like her father, and while their relationship was oddly formal for a parent and child there was really no doubt about their genetic bond.

Maybe there wasn't anything too odd about their interaction either. Samantha's face lit up at the sight of her father's smile and the look that passed between the pair suggested a genuine closeness. Warmth, even. Felicity had the fleeting and rather disturbing thought that she would like just such a look directed at her from this man.

She excused herself hurriedly. She had no time to ponder the intricacies of this particular family's relationships with each other and she certainly didn't want to be distracted by any peculiar reactions to Joe. There were other patients waiting to be seen.

The potential heart-attack patient from out of town had arrived in the department. Felicity accompanied the man during his rapid transfer to a resuscitation area. Geoffrey Pinnington was a forty-year-old farmer from a rural area well north of the city.

'I'd been feeling a few niggles all morning,' he told Felicity in response to her first query. 'I thought I must have pulled a muscle, heaving hay bales around. I'd just finished my lunch when I started feeling really terrible. I went all sweaty and lost my lunch and this awful pain started up.'

'Where was the pain?'

'Right here.' Geoffrey slapped a hand on the centre of his chest. The nurse attending to the 12-lead electrocardiogram hastily reattached a dislodged electrode.

'Try and keep still for a moment, please, Mr Pinnington,' the nurse requested.

'Was the pain just in the one spot?' Felicity asked.

'No. It went into my neck and then all the way down my left arm.'

'Given a scale of zero to ten, with zero being no pain and ten being the worst you could imagine, what score would you have given it?'

'Twelve.' Geoffrey smiled wryly. 'I've never felt so bad in my life. I really thought I was about to die.'

Felicity nodded sympathetically. A feeling of impending doom was a common symptom of a heart attack. 'What time did the pain come on?'

'One o'clock or thereabouts. Maybe a quarter past.'

'OK.' Felicity glanced at her watch. Nearly three hours ago. They were still well within the therapeutic window for an angioplasty procedure which could abort the damage being caused by the lack of coronary blood flow.

'Give Cardiology a call,' she directed the registrar beside her. Felicity picked up the ECG trace and scanned it rapidly. The changes were abnormal and clear-cut. 'Tell them we have a probable anterior infarct in progress here.' She turned to the junior doctor who was drawing blood from the IV line already in Geoffrey's arm. 'We need cardiac enzymes, CBC, electrolytes and lipids done, Sarah.' Her attention returned to her patient. 'How's the pain at the moment?'

'Not too bad. The stuff the GP gave me was good.'

Felicity nodded. She'd read the ambulance patient report form as she'd walked into the resuscitation area. After a half-hour drive to the local doctor, Geoffrey had been given treatment consisting of oxygen, pain relief, an anti-nausea agent, aspirin and GTN. The general practioner had then called for an ambulance for urgent transfer to hospital. All the right things had been done and the GP's note included baseline measurements and a brief medical history that didn't indicate any risk factors for heart disease. But Felicity wanted to double-check.

'So you've never had any problems with your heart before this, Geoffrey?'

'No.'

'No other medical conditions you're treated for?'

'No, nothing.'

'Blood pressure's always been OK?'

'As far as I know.'

'Have you ever had your cholesterol levels checked?'

Geoffrey nodded. 'Always been fine. I'm fit and healthy, Doctor, and I'm far too young to be having a heart attack, aren't I?'

'Unfortunately there are always exceptions to the general rules. Is there any history of heart disease in your family?'

'My dad gets chest pain sometimes, I reckon. He's one of the old school and wouldn't admit to it, but I've seen him rubbing his chest and looking a bit grey sometimes.'

'Do you smoke?'

'Used to. I knocked it on the head a couple of years ago.'

'Good for you.' Felicity had enough information to transfer this patient directly to Cardiology. Baseline measurements and recordings had all been completed by the team in the resus area. When the curtain was drawn back behind her she expected the new arrival to be the cardiology registrar. Instead, it was a woman with two young children beside her.

'Sorry, Geoff. I couldn't drive as fast as the ambulance. How are you feeling?'

'Not too bad, love. Don't worry.' Geoffrey smiled at his wife. He winked at his son who was about ten years old but the boy was staring, wide-eyed, at the screens of the monitoring equipment. The younger child, a girl, was clutching her mother's hand, staring at her father and crying quietly.

'It's OK, chicken,' Geoffrey said gently. 'Dad's going to be just fine.' He held out the arm that wasn't encumbered by IV tubing and the girl ducked behind a nurse and rushed into the inviting circle, burying her face against her father's chest. Mrs Pinnington also moved closer and laid her hand on Geoffrey's leg. Felicity watched as the family drew themselves into a unit again, preparing to cope with whatever was coming next. She answered the querying look Geoffrey's wife was directing towards her.

'It looks as though Geoffrey may be having a heart attack,' Felicity explained. 'There's a cardiologist on the way to see him now and they'll decide what the best course of treatment will be. You've done exactly the right thing in getting Geoffrey to the doctor and into hospital as quickly as possible. That means the treatment has much more chance of being successful and that any damage that is occurring can be minimised.'

The cardiology registrar arrived while Felicity was talking. She took over the management of the patient but Felicity stayed in the resus area, listening and watching, for a few minutes. The registrar assimilated the available information quickly. She explained the mechanics of the life-threatening condition Geoffrey was experiencing and outlined the treatment options. Felicity watched as he listened carefully. His daughter was still tucked within his arm and he was stroking her hair. Blonde, straight hair. Not at all like Samantha Petersen's.

Given the choice between drug therapy and the more invasive but faster and probably more effective procedure of angioplasty, the Pinningtons had no difficulty making a choice, and the staff prepared to move Geoffrey upstairs to the catheter laboratory. It was time for Felicity to move as well. With no urgent cases awaiting her attention, she collected a cup of cold water and stood observing the department for a minute from her position beside the water dispenser. She wasn't really registering the activity in the department, however. She was still thinking about Geoffrey and his daughter. Or, more specifically, the interaction between them and the contrast it had presented to the way Joe and Samantha had appeared. That easy affection and physical closeness had been non-existent.

Sometimes the frightening environment of an emergency department made people act oddly, but Joe was a surgeon. He should have been as much at home here as anywhere, and more capable of reassuring his daughter than most people. On reflection, it was hard to believe that the pair were father and daughter. The atmosphere of awkwardness was more like that of a relative or care-giver being thrown into dealing with an unfortunate and unexpected incident. A care-giver who only had limited contact with children, perhaps.

Felicity crumpled the polystyrene cup and threw it away. Maybe Joe was just a father who couldn't be bothered and left the upbringing of his children entirely to his wife. Or maybe he had been missing an important appointment because of the accident. What did it matter anyway? It was really none of her business. Instinct had already told her that the unusual atmosphere was highly unlikely to be due to some dysfunctional or abusive relationship that needed further investigation so Felicity was slightly annoyed at her continuing level of interest.

No distractions were immediately available in the department.

'I'll be in my office,' she told Mike. 'I've got some paperwork to catch up on. Beep me if you need me.'

The left turn at the doors into the main part of the hospital took Felicity past the store cupboards, the sluice room and the relatives' room on her right. The bed coming from the observation ward on the other side of the corridor slowed her decisive walk for only a few moments, but it was long enough to recognise the voices coming from the area set aside for relatives. One of the voices, at least.

'For God's sake, Joe. I just can't understand how it could have happened!'

Joe had had almost enough. The day had already been a disaster and Dayna was just making things worse.

'I told you, Dayna. It was an accident. She missed her footing when she jumped off the swing. She fell over. Accidents happen.'

'I would have thought you could manage a simple trip to the park without some sort of disaster.' Dayna's tone was scathing. 'This is just typical of you, Joe. How bad is it?'

Joe sighed. It was typical. Dayna expected any time he spent with Samantha to cause problems and no matter how hard he tried her expectation always seemed to be justified. Usually it was something minor like stained clothing from a spilled drink or a damaged toy—things that Dayna could have ignored easily enough if she chose to. He had to concede that a broken arm wasn't something to dismiss lightly.

'It's a greenstick fracture.'

'What on earth is that?'

'It's where the bone doesn't break completely. One side breaks and the other side gets bent. It happens commonly with children.' Joe frowned. 'For heaven's sake, Dayna. It's exactly what Scott did to his arm a couple of years ago.'

'He's a boy.' Dayna clearly dismissed the reference to her older son's injury as unimportant. 'Where is Samantha, Joe? I hope you haven't left her sitting somewhere by herself.'

'Of course I haven't. She has a nurse with her.'

'Well, I want to see her. Now.'

'Of course.' Joe stood back to let his sister-in-law exit the small room first. He followed, edging past the bed being manoeuvred awkwardly in the corridor outside. Another sigh escaped him. Just how much of Dayna's rather heated conversation had been overheard by Dr Felicity Munroe? And why was she standing there at this particular moment anyway?

Joe led Dayna towards the emergency department. He was still appalled at having discovered Felicity's qualifications and position. The fleeting memories of things he had said to her on the building site had made him cringe inwardly. Fancy suggesting that a consultant in emergency medicine might not know what she was doing and cause further damage. Or suggesting that if she wanted to be useful she could hold the head still. Of course, she could have told him she was a doctor but Joe had a sneaking suspicion that she had been right in saying she hadn't been given much of an opportunity. The scene had reminded him too strongly of Catherine's accident and the ghastly aftermath of a mismanaged spinal injury. He hadn't been about to allow anyone to interfere with what he knew to be expert leadership.

Joe pulled back the curtain to cubicle 3. If only he hadn't compounded the error by assuming that Felicity Munroe was a nurse when she'd arrived to look after Samantha. If he hadn't been so worried about his daughter he might have noticed that she hadn't been wearing a uniform. He might have taken the trouble to read the identity badge pinned to the waistband of her skirt.

'Hello, Mum.' Samantha was smiling. 'Look at my arm plaster. It's pink!'

'Very pretty.' The nurse beside the bed stepped back as Dayna leaned over to kiss Samantha. 'Does it hurt a lot, darling?'

'Not any more. I had some medicine. I'm hungry now.'

Joe smiled at Samantha. She was looking a lot happier. All that he needed now was some more time with her and he could probably wipe out the unpleasant aspects of their outing. 'Maybe we could go out for a hamburger.'

'No,' Dayna said firmly. 'It's time to go home.'

Samantha looked disappointed enough to prompt Joe to try again. 'I could drop Sam home a bit later.'

'I've come into the hospital now, Joe. I've left the boys with Nigel and he's busy at work. We've got grocery shopping to do and Scott's due at his piano lesson at 4:30. I haven't got time to chop and change arrangements. I'll take Samantha home with me now.'

Joe gave in. It wasn't worth the stress of trying to talk Dayna out of a decision. Not this time anyway, when Samantha was probably tired. He watched Dayna help his daughter off the bed.

'Mum?'

Dayna was folding up Samantha's cardigan, which had been abandoned on the end of the bed. She didn't appear to have heard.

'Mum?'

Joe gritted his teeth at the repetition. Dayna wasn't Samantha's mother. She was her aunt. Samantha had started calling her 'Mum' because of the example set by Dayna's two sons. And Dayna certainly hadn't discouraged her.

'Mum?' Samantha was trying again. 'Can I give Woof Woof Snowball a bath with me tonight? He's really dirty.'

'He can go in the washing machine.' Dayna turned her attention to the nurse who required a signature on the discharge papers. Joe bent down towards his daughter and spoke quietly.

'When you come and stay with me you can give Woof Woof Snowball a real bath.'

Samantha's grin at the private suggestion was worth a lot. The one-armed hug was worth even more, despite the obstacle the soft toy presented. It almost restored the pleasure Joe had anticipated from the afternoon's outing. He could watch Dayna lead Samantha briskly away without the usual heartache. He even found himself smiling. Using that awful name for the toy hadn't been that difficult at all. Maybe he just needed to relax. He just hadn't had enough time with his daughter and that wasn't entirely his fault.

He could learn. Look at how easily Felicity had established such an easy rapport with his child. Instead of being resentful at the way she'd effortlessly gained what he was having such difficulty achieving, he should follow her example. He could be relaxed and confident like that. And friendly. Felicity was obviously a friendly person, good with children, and she clearly knew what she was doing if she was a consultant emergency physician. She looked far too young for the position. She couldn't be much over thirty, surely?

It seemed, by now, typical that Joe should encounter Felicity as he left the emergency department. This woman had a knack of appearing when least expected. He paused and directed a smile at her.

'Thanks very much for your help, Dr Munroe.'

'A pleasure, Dr Petersen.'

The formality was ridiculous. It made them both smile.

'The name's Joe.'

'And mine's Fliss.'

They both held their hands out simultaneously. The shake was brief but firm. Not so brief that Joe didn't notice that Felicity wasn't wearing a wedding ring, however. His mind was turning rapidly. No, she couldn't be much over thirty and she really was an incredibly attractive woman. Those large hazel eyes were rather difficult to look away from. They weren't looking as friendly as they had when Samantha had been around but that was hardly surprising.

'I'd like to apologise,' he found himself saying hurriedly.

'What for?' Felicity's tone was cool. Disinterested, perhaps?

What for, indeed. There was too much to choose from. Joe had insulted her on more than one occasion already by making erroneous assumptions about her qualifications. He'd also displayed his lack of confident parenting in an embarrassing manner. He should have known better than to answer

Samantha's questions for her. Or upset her about the dog's name. Felicity probably thought he was an idiot. A rude idiot, at that.

'Our acquaintance didn't get off to the best start. I'm sorry I didn't enlist your expertise at that accident scene.'

'You didn't know I had any.' Felicity dismissed the apology.

'I wasn't much of a help with Samantha today either.'

'It's often harder to cope with one's own family than patients.'

'The thing is, I...' Joe hesitated. The only hope he had of repairing this woman's opinion of him would require her to have at least some understanding of the complicated background his actions sprang from. However, any explanation of the reasons for his behaviour on the two occasions they'd met was likely to be time-consuming, and Felicity was looking past Joe's shoulder at present as though she wanted to escape. 'I'd just like a chance to explain,' Joe finished. 'An opportunity to redeem myself, perhaps.'

'There's absolutely no need.'

'Maybe a coffee?' Joe couldn't quite accept the brush-off. He didn't want to be brushed off. 'When you have the time, that is.'

'I don't think so.' Felicity's smile was polite.

'But thanks for the invitation. Nice meeting you again, Joe.'

Joe watched Felicity walk into the emergency department and kicked himself mentally. Surely he could have handled that a bit better. He had really wanted that coffee. It would have provided the opportunity to spend time with the young doctor and gain more than the initial impression he was being left with. It was an impression he was not going to forget in a hurry. One that he would very much have liked to have built on.

Not that he was going to get the chance. Felicity had spelt that out fairly convincingly. Of course, there was always that appointment Joe had tomorrow. If that interview was successful it was just possible he might get another opportunity to persuade Felicity that he was worth spending some time with. He hadn't been all that bothered about whether it was going to be successful because he hadn't been sure it was what he really wanted. Now Joe was quite sure it was what he wanted.

He wanted it rather a lot.

CHAPTER THREE

'WHAT on earth is taking so long?'

'I have no idea.'

Felicity frowned at her watch. 'How long is it since you put in the call for the neurosurgical registrar?'

'Must be nearly ten minutes.' Emergency Department Registrar Colin White looked worried. 'They said he was just finishing a case in the operating theatre and would be here directly.'

'Ten minutes is a long way from "directly".' Felicity's glance raked the monitor screens surrounding the trauma room bed. 'I think we'll just transfer her to CT scanning now. We've got two multi-trauma patients from a motor vehicle accident coming in by helicopter with an estimated time of arrival of eight minutes. We need to get this room cleared.'

Felicity's gaze was on the unconscious woman on the bed as the door to the trauma room swung open. She didn't waver from her visual reassessment and mental review of the patient as the newcomer joined the team at the bedside.

'Hi. I'm the neurosurgical registrar. Joe Petersen.'

Felicity had never looked up so quickly in her life. For a split second she was totally distracted from the case she was managing. Her patient could have been on another planet. It had been three weeks since Joe had appeared in the emergency department with his daughter. She had forgotten about him…almost. Not only had he stepped back into her world, he was now standing on the other side of a critically ill patient whose care they needed to co-operate over professionally. Felicity snapped the lid closed on her stunned reaction.

'This is Crystal Loftman,' she informed Joe crisply. 'Fifty-six years old, previously fit woman with no prior history and on no medications. She complained of severe head and neck pain, vomited once and then collapsed approximately twenty-five minutes ago.'

Joe was making his own visual assessment of the obese woman lying on the bed.

'Vital signs on arrival?' he queried.

Joe wanted the baseline measurements that would give an indication of the patient's condition on her arrival in the emergency department. Felicity's verbal report covered a normal heart rate and rhythm and a normal blood pressure. The woman's pupils had been of equal size and had showed an expected constriction when exposed to bright light. Her breathing rate had been high and the level of consciousness well down. Crystal Loftman had not been able to open her eyes or give anything more than an incoherent verbal response to questions. Joe was watching the monitors as he listened to Felicity's succinct summary. He noted that the blood-pressure reading had changed and was now showing a greater difference between the systolic and diastolic readings. The change could be significant and indicate rising intracranial pressure.

'Blood-glucose level?' Joe moved to the patient's head. He held her left eyelid open as he shone a bright penlight on the pupil to check the reaction to light.

'Six point five.' Ruling out an abnormal blood sugar level as a cause for a lowered level of consciousness was a standard procedure. It had been done by ambulance staff on the scene.

'Why is she intubated?'

The tube that had been placed in the patient's airway and the equipment now controlling her breathing had been necessary because of the continued vomiting she had been experiencing. Felicity had done the intubation herself as quickly as possible and was happy to justify the procedure. Complications from aspiration of vomit could be disastrous and Crystal's level of consciousness made the potential risk very high.

'Has a CT scan been booked?'

'They're ready for her now.' Colin White joined the conversation between Felicity and Joe.

Joe nodded. 'Let's go, then.'

Felicity's decisive nod mirrored Joe's. He had been in the room for less than two minutes and the flurry of activity indicated the staff's readiness for a rapid transfer of their patient to the next stage of her assessment and treatment. The handover to the appropriate department was completed and Felicity watched Joe accompany the bed as it was wheeled from the trauma room. A small cluster of extra staff were part of the procession as they carried or supervised the attached monitoring systems.

The flash of satisfaction was normal. Felicity knew that she had done her best for Crystal and the trauma room would be ready within minutes to receive the next cases requiring urgent attention. The flash of a quite different sensation was definitely not normal. It could have been easily ignored except that Felicity stepped out of the trauma room in time to see the group of staff rearrange their positions slightly as their patient's bed was manoeuvred through the doors to the main hospital. Joe chose that moment to glance back into the emergency department and his gaze met that of Felicity. She turned away abruptly.

What did she feel? Irritation at the surprise of Joe's appearance? Suspicion of a new colleague who had yet to prove his ability? Felicity smiled wryly. OK, so she had good reason to believe his professional ability might be up to scratch, given his management of that spinal injury patient. She also had good reason to believe that he might have an arrogant tendency to assume control and patronise the abilities of others. That would not be a desirable attribute in any colleague. Felicity's smile faded, leaving her face thoughtful as she approached the sorting desk to confirm the ETA of the expected car-accident victims.

Joe was working as a registrar—a temporary position with definite limits on making clinical decisions. She was a consultant—a permanent position with an implied trust in her clinical judgement that allowed her to direct the actions of her registrars. Including those of neurosurgical registrars—at least while they were working in her department. Not only did Joe now know who she was, he would have to do what she told him to do. Felicity's smile returned briefly and inwardly. She hadn't enjoyed being treated as an attractive but relatively useless assistant at that accident scene. She hadn't enjoyed the assumption that she was a nurse when they'd met again in the emergency department, and she had definitely not appreciated being asked out for coffee by a man whose wife and child had been virtually within earshot. Maybe that flash of sensation when she looked at Joe was, in fact, pleasure at the potential opportunity to repay him for his inappropriate attitude and invitation.

The opportunity didn't arise again during the remainder of Felicity's shift, although Joe did return to the department at 9 p.m. Felicity hadn't been invited to join the group of junior staff surrounding a row of X-ray viewing screens but she paused anyway. Joe had illuminated a series of CT scan images and was pointing out the abnormalities to some of the trauma team staff.

'You can see the large amount of blood within the ventricles. Significant amount of ventricular dilatation as well.' His finger traced the shadowy outline of the brain's structures which the CT scanning had revealed. His hand moved to another screen.

'She's got pools of blood in several other places as well. See here? And here?'

'What's being done for her in the intensive care unit?' a nurse queried.

'We've put in a right-sided ventricular drain,' Joe responded, 'to try and clear the accumulation of blood. But she's suffered a catastrophic subarachnoid haemorrhage and the prognosis isn't wonderful. We'll make a decision regarding surgery first thing in the morning.'

Joe didn't notice Felicity's presence until the small group dispersed. When he did, his smile was appealing. 'I hope you don't mind me disrupting your staff, Fliss. I thought they might be interested in some follow-up.'

'I don't mind at all. Follow-up is always appreciated, especially by the nurses. They tend to get left out of the loop sometimes.' Felicity moved on. While the extra visit would certainly have been appreciated, she wasn't about to encourage Joe to spend more time than necessary in her department.

Joe intended to make the most of every opportunity he got to spend time in the emergency department. He was walking in that very direction at the moment. His first full night shift marked the start of his third week as Queen Mary's neurosurgical registrar. He hadn't actually been called to the department but things were quiet and he wanted to leave a report on a patient from a couple of days ago. Staff members were getting used to his habit of providing follow-up and someone had specifically requested an update on this patient. It was after 11 p.m. so Joe knew he was unlikely to receive the huge bonus of seeing Felicity but he also knew that wouldn't stop him watching out for her...and hoping.

He was doing it now as he walked the corridors of the main hospital. He did it when he was in the cafeteria. Hell, he even did it in the damned car-parking building. Despite the short length of time he had been practising this activity, Joe had become an expert in recognising that lithe figure and graceful walk from any distance. He could pick the soft lilt of her voice from the babble of conversations around surrounding tables in the cafeteria and he never failed to instantly recognise the delicious gurgle of her laughter.

Not that she laughed knowingly in his presence. She didn't even smile very often, but that didn't stop Joe watching for the dimple that appeared in her left cheek when she did. Given the major issues in his life that had drawn Joe back to New Zealand, he was amazed that he had allowed a complication like this to develop, but it was way beyond any control he could exert now. Never in his life had Joe met such an attractive woman.

Felicity was tall—only a few inches below his own height of six-two. Her long, straight hair was a rich shade of brown, just a little darker than the warm hazel of her eyes. Her physical appearance was only a small part of the package, however. Felicity exuded a calm confidence that Joe now knew to be matched by a professional competency that had the young consultant held in high regard by everyone who worked with her.

It had taken a few weeks for the embarrassment of having treated her first as a layperson and then as a nurse to fade, but Joe was sure they had got past that unfortunate beginning. They would probably find it hilarious one of these days. That was, if he could just find a way of getting close enough to have an even remotely personal interaction with this elusive woman.

Joe nodded and smiled at the group of nurses passing him on their way back from a meal break in the cafeteria. He knew several of them by name now. It had been surprisingly easy to fit in with the friendly working environment in his new job. He could probably strike up more than a casual acquaintance with one of those nurses if he wanted to. But there was only one person Joe Petersen was interested in getting to know, and it was proving depressingly difficult.

Heaven knew, he had tried hard enough. At times he thought he was making progress. Like the day after that first cerebrovascular case when he'd startled Felicity by appearing as the neurosurgical registrar on call. He'd been called in to assess a child with moderate concussion that time and he'd deliberately hung around, taking his time with the paperwork because Felicity had been checking something on a computer screen nearby. It had been Felicity who'd initiated the conversation that time, but maybe she'd been as aware as he had of their proximity and lack of interaction.

'Did you ever hear any follow-up on that young

man who fell from the scaffolding?' The query was polite but Joe hoped he wasn't imagining the genuine desire to talk to him.

'Jeff Simms?' His response was eager. 'I've been out to see him a couple of times actually. I'm very impressed by the set up at Coronation Hospital.'

Felicity's nod was brisk. She clearly agreed with his assessment of the specialist spinal injury centre on the western side of Christchurch city, but she was more interested in his report on the patient concerned. 'So, how is he doing? Was it a complete spinal cord lesion?'

'Unfortunately, yes. Below C5. He's tetraplegic.' Joe had shaken his head. 'He was in a bad way for the first week. Neurogenic shock and paralytic ileus gave him respiratory complications and he had to be tubed and ventilated for a while. He got a respiratory infection on top of that but he's coming right now. Physically, anyway. It's going to take a long time to come to terms with the injury.'

'Poor kid.' Felicity seemed genuinely distressed. 'I doubt that anyone really comes to terms with that kind of disability. Not when it's such an instant and catastrophic change.'

'It's certainly very difficult.' Joe abandoned his notes, sitting back in his chair, delighted with the prospect of continuing the conversation.

If only Felicity hadn't been called away to the

woman with the erratic heartbeat. And if only he hadn't tried to rush things by suggesting they meet for a coffee after work.

Talk about conflicting signals. She'd looked tempted for an instant there but that had changed instantly into a look that had suggested he'd not just overstepped the mark—he'd flown past straight into the sin bin. What had been so wrong with asking her out for a coffee? Was there some house rule about not getting to know your colleagues on a personal level? Hardly likely. Maybe Felicity was married and didn't wear her ring to work. That was far more likely and Joe had used his next visit to Emergency a few days later to conduct that important piece of detective work.

Gareth Harvey, the senior emergency department consultant, had made it easy. Well respected for his long-term leadership and success in demanding improvements in Queen Mary's emergency department, Gareth was still an approachable and fatherly figure. Joe had been pleased when Gareth had taken the time to welcome him onto the staff and compliment his management of a complicated fracture case he had attended.

'I had help with that fracture,' Joe responded. 'The nerve damage would have been a lot more severe if the initial management hadn't been so good.'

He paused only fractionally. 'Felicity Munroe is a very competent young doctor.'

'Fliss is fantastic,' Gareth agreed readily. 'We're lucky to have her. She's our newest consultant and one of the best. I hope she'll be here for a long time.'

'Why wouldn't she be?'

'She may want some more overseas experience at some stage. There's no reason why she can't take her career in any direction she wants, and postgraduate qualifications are sometimes best done in more internationally recognised centres.' Gareth gave Joe a rather speculative glance. 'Then again, young female doctors—especially when they look like Fliss—have been known to get lured into marriage and whisked away.' He chuckled. 'Usually by another young doctor wanting some overseas experience.'

'Oh.' Joe pretended a nonchalance he definitely didn't feel. 'So there's some young doctor waiting in the wings to whisk Felicity away?'

'Not that I know of.' The twitch of one eye that accompanied the smile was almost a wink. Joe received the message that if Felicity had a significant relationship of some kind then Gareth would very likely know about it.

So she wasn't married and it was commonplace for colleagues to get close enough to marry each

other and disappear overseas. Maybe Felicity had a
personal objection to a relationship with a colleague,
but that was no problem. For a start he was mostly
in another department and his position was hope-
fully only temporary. Joe had his sights set on a
consultant position at Coronation Hospital. His follow-up on Jeff Simms had carried the bonus of
meeting the staff at the spinal unit. Approval for a
new consultant position was being sought right now.
The job could well be advertised in the not-so-
distant future.

Maybe the problem was just that Felicity didn't
find him as attractive as he found her. Joe had to
concede that was probable and he couldn't expect
his overwhelming response to be reciprocated. Not
unless he was the luckiest man on earth. All he
wanted was an indication that there was some interest. Enough to start something that might develop
into what his instincts told him would be the most
exciting prospect his life had so far offered him. He
had loved Catherine. Of course he had. But Joe
couldn't remember ever feeling quite *this* strongly
about her.

It couldn't be solely his imagination that had con-
jured up the impression that Felicity found him at
least intriguing, if not actually attractive. He knew
she watched him whenever he was engaged in ac-
tivities in her department. He could feel the intensity

with which she observed his management of any case they shared. Joe had been aware of that the first time they'd met. He'd been slightly irritated by the scrutiny he'd known he'd been under from the woman holding Jeff's head, but he'd dismissed it as simply bystander fascination with trauma management.

Three weeks into his new job, Joe had the satisfaction of knowing that Felicity was as impressed by his professional competency as he was by hers. Mutual respect, however, wasn't enough of a basis on which to have built the hopes that Joe now entertained, and that hope wouldn't have continued to grow if he hadn't detected something more.

The frequent eye contact was certainly not coincidental. Or unilateral. Felicity might be the first to look away every time their eyes met but that couldn't negate the fact that she *had* been looking. She was watching his approach now. Maybe she was expecting the usual professional exchange the staff had come to expect from Joe's surprise visits. The unexpected pleasure of finding Felicity on night duty was enough to prompt Joe into taking yet another risk of rejection.

'How's your dog?' he asked casually, after greeting Felicity. 'Rusty, isn't it?'

She wasn't quick enough to disguise her pleased

surprise. 'How on earth did you remember something like that?'

'Hard not to.' Joe's grin was genuinely amused. 'I find myself thinking about Irish setter tails whenever I'm brushing my daughter's hair.'

The shutters came down. 'How is Samantha?' Felicity queried politely. 'Is the cast off her arm now?'

'It has been for a while. The fracture's completely healed. Sam's forgotten all about it.'

'That's good.' Felicity seemed less than interested. She responded quickly to a signal from her pager that Joe recognised as being the summons for the trauma team.

He watched her walk away. Was that it? Was it the fact that he had a child that put Felicity off? Did she hate kids? No. Nobody could hate children and be able to establish the kind of rapport that had sprung up so quickly between Felicity and Samantha. Maybe Felicity wanted her own children and not someone else's. That was understandably offputting but Joe wasn't defeated. Samantha was a lovable kid. She could win anyone's heart if they knew her well enough. His daughter wouldn't present a major barrier to a relationship. She wasn't even living with him at the moment, for heaven's sake. It was simply a matter of overcoming the first obstacle and persuading Felicity that it was worth spending a little time with him. That was the only way he would find out whether this intense interest was simply infatuation or the seeds of something really significant.

The automatic doors to the ambulance bay opened and Joe saw a stretcher being wheeled directly to the trauma room. He noted the blood-stained dressing on the accident victim's head and moved closer. There wasn't much point in leaving the department only to be summoned back to assess a head injury. Joe stood just inside the doors to the trauma room, well out of the way of the team working around the central table.

The patient was a young man. He was conscious and distressed.

'I'm Fliss Munroe,' Felicity told him. 'I'm one of the doctors here. What's your name?'

'Chris Keen. Can somebody call my mother?'

'Try and keep this on.' Felicity replaced the oxygen mask that Chris had pulled away from his face. 'Do you know where you are, Chris?'

'I'm in the hospital. Please—my mum's number is 2736 4519. Can you call her?'

'Someone's contacting her now, Chris. Try and keep still for us. We need to find out how much damage you've done to yourself.'

Felicity replaced the oxygen mask again. Other staff were having difficulty attaching a blood-pressure cuff and ECG electrodes. An IV line had been pulled out and needed replacing urgently. Joe could hear the respiratory difficulty the youth was in. The breathing rate was fast and noisy. He could also see that the oxygen saturation level was well down but Chris was too agitated to tolerate the mask on his face. Gareth was trying to listen to the patient's chest with a stethoscope. Joe knew how difficult the assessment must be, given that Chris hadn't stopped talking. At least he was alert and appeared oriented. Maybe the head injury wasn't too serious, although the repetitive statements indicated a significant concussion. He had told the staff his mother's telephone number at least four times now. When his clothing was cut away, extensive injuries to the left side of the body, including the chest wall, were revealed.

Joe watched Felicity and Gareth manage the difficult task of inserting a chest drain in an agitated patient. The procedure improved the respiratory distress and the young man's agitation began to recede. Was that because of the improved oxygen delivery, though? Joe focused more sharply. Maybe it was due more to a declining level of consciousness.

The survey to check for any other life-threatening injuries or blood loss took another minute and Joe used the opportunity to speak to the paramedic who had stayed to observe the resuscitation of the patient he'd brought in. Joe was pleased to remember his name.

'Hi, Stan. What happened to Chris?'

'Motorbike versus tree. He lost control on a bend thanks to the wet conditions.'

'Was he wearing a helmet?'

Stanley nodded. 'It's got quite a dent in it and he was unconscious for at least five minutes according to a witness. He was very confused initially and quite combative.'

'Any obvious skull fracture?'

Stanley nodded again. 'Depressed fracture in the left parietal area.'

'Open?'

'No. The bleeding's come from a scalp laceration. Left pupil was sluggish but he became more responsive and co-operative *en route*.' Stanley shook his head sadly. 'I wish I'd taped up that IV line a bit better. I hate it when they get yanked out.'

Joe was watching the monitors. The pulse pressure had widened in the last couple of minutes and the heart rate had dropped from a tachycardia of 130 to a rate of 95. The respiration rate had also dropped markedly and Chris Keen's level of consciousness was still dropping. Was it an effect of the narcotic analgesia that had been administered or the sign of something more sinister?

'Chris?' Felicity spoke loudly. 'Open your eyes

for me.' She shone a small torch onto his pupils. The eyelids drifted shut quickly. 'Left pupil is dilating,' Felicity announced. She cast another glance at the changes on the monitors. 'I think we have a head injury going off here.' She looked at Gareth who nodded his agreement.

'What do you want to do, Fliss?'

'I think we should sedate and intubate. And let's get someone down from Neurosurgery, stat.'

'I'm here already.' Joe stepped forward and was rewarded with a quick grin from Felicity.

'I can't complain about how long that took. How much have you caught up on what's going on here?'

'Enough.' Joe pulled on gloves before removing the dressing to examine their patient's head. The skull was definitely fractured. The left pupil was now fixed and dilated. The pulse pressure had widened further and the heart rate was dropping rapidly and becoming irregular. Chris was now unresponsive to verbal stimuli.

'What do you think, Joe? Have we got time to scan him and get him to Theatre?'

'We may not have time to get Theatre even set up at the rate his intracranial pressure seems to be climbing. Have you got the gear for burr holes down here?'

Felicity's eyes widened. 'Of course. I've never

seen it done in the emergency department before, though.'

'First time for everything.' Joe raised an eyebrow towards Gareth. 'Are you happy if I go ahead? Would you rather try and call in one of the consultant neurosurgeons?'

Gareth shook his head. 'There's no time for that and, from what I've been told, you're rather over-qualified to be a registrar in the first place. I agree with you. We can't afford to lose even minutes here.'

The trauma room team swung quickly into action under Joe's direction. An intravenous infusion of mannitol was started to treat any swelling of brain tissue. Further intravenous access was gained with the insertion of a subclavian central venous line and blood for transfusion was ordered. A general anaesthetic was administered and ventilation equipment took over Chris's breathing. His head was shaved and painted with disinfectant and the rest of his body covered with sterile drapes. Felicity scrubbed and gowned up to assist Joe with the emergency surgical procedure.

Joe made his first incision confidently, moving upwards from just in front of the ear. 'There's the temporal artery,' he pointed out. 'Clamp that, will you, please, Fliss?'

Joe used the scalpel again to sever the muscles

and a retractor to hold them apart. The thin membrane covering the skull was scraped away to leave an exposed area of bone ready for Joe to use the drill to create a burr hole. Felicity held her breath as she watched Joe using the surgical power tool. It required enormous skill to know just how far to go.

'Look at that.' Joe sounded satisfied as he inspected the completed hole. Felicity could see the blue colour and tension of the exposed dura membrane covering Chris's brain. They were getting closer to the source of the life-threatening bleeding.

'We need to enlarge this burr hole, open the dura and get as much of the clot out as we can. Then we'll see what we can do about locating the bleeding point.'

'He's losing a lot of blood,' Felicity warned.

'Don't worry about that for the moment,' Joe responded calmly. 'Death from brain compression is a lot faster.'

Joe's outward calm during the next few minutes effectively concealed the fact that they were as tense as any he had experienced during his many years of surgery. The life of a young man was at stake here and his performance was critical. He used the burr drill again to make more holes in the skull. A fine wire saw enabled the bone between the holes to be cut and a small flap of bone to be removed. He cut the dura with scissors and removed a large clot of blood so that the arterial bleed that had caused the crisis was visible. Then he tied off the damaged section to control the continuing haemorrhage.

His own relief was reflected on every face in the trauma team, particularly that of Felicity. As the monitors confirmed the improvement in their patient's condition, the relief was also tinged with a palpable admiration that Joe tried to shrug off.

'I'll go with him up to Theatre,' he informed the team.

'Let us know how he gets on, won't you?' Felicity paused. 'You did really well there, Joe. I was impressed.'

'Thanks.' He couldn't shrug that accolade off. He smiled at Felicity. 'I'll be back later. Maybe I can even earn a coffee in exchange for an update.'

She returned the smile. 'I'm sure that could be arranged. How long will the surgery take?'

'We'll need to check that the bleeding is completely controlled, replace the bone flap and close up. Then it will depend on what we find around that fracture, but it shouldn't be too long. What time does your shift finish?'

'Seven a.m.'

Joe's smile was still hovering as he accompanied Chris Keen out of the emergency department. It was just after midnight now. Even if he was tied up with his patient for the next two or three hours, there would still be plenty of time to see Felicity. With a bit of luck the department might be nice and quiet at that time of night. Maybe they wouldn't be alone, having their coffee, but beggars couldn't be choosers. It was a start.

Joe hoped that the emergency department staffroom was equipped with really big coffee-mugs.

CHAPTER FOUR

THE emergency department was virtually deserted.

Had Felicity been waiting for him to come back? There was no obvious reason for her to be standing near one of the resus areas. The intensive treatment rooms were all unoccupied as were most of the cubicles. A junior doctor and two nurses were looking after what looked liked a couple of minor cases. There was no doubt that Felicity's expression was welcoming when she spotted Joe's approach.

'Hi, Joe. You've been ages. How's Mr Keen?'

'Doing fine. I've just left ICU. He's breathing on his own and cerebral oedema is well controlled so far. It'll be a day or two before we can really assess for any neurological damage but my guess is that he's going to be OK.'

'That's great.' Felicity's smile was wide. 'I suppose I owe you that coffee now.'

'Sure do.'

'If there's any left, that is. Most of the staff are in there. It's not often we get a night as quiet as this. It's been quite boring since you left.'

'Too much excitement isn't good for you.' Joe

grinned. 'Burr holes are probably enough for one night.'

'It *was* exciting.' Felicity led the way to the staffroom. 'And I'm so pleased it was successful.'

Not half as pleased as he was, Joe suspected. It had proved to be a bit of a coup as far as getting Felicity's attention went, but that wouldn't have been the case if the procedure had failed. It was just a shame he was going to have to share her company now with most of the department.

As expected, the chairs around the staffroom table were all occupied. Nurses, aides, student doctors and registrars were drinking coffee, flicking through magazines and engaging in sporadic bursts of conversation that reflected a general level of weariness. Not exactly a conducive atmosphere for the kind of personal conversation Joe wanted. His disappointment faded, however, as Felicity led him to the far end of the room where the collection of armchairs was deserted, apart from the one in the corner, where Colin was sound asleep and snoring softly.

Felicity smiled as she sat down. 'Colin looks a lot cuter when he's asleep.'

'Kids are like that.' Joe sat down in the chair beside Felicity's. 'No matter how badly behaved they've been, they look like angels as soon as the Zs hit.' He sipped his coffee and sighed with appreciation. 'That's good,' he announced. 'It's been a long night.'

The glance towards Felicity was curious. 'Have you got any children, Fliss?'

'I'm not married.'

Joe's grin was mischievous. 'Being married and having children aren't mutually exclusive as far as I've observed.'

'OK—no, I haven't got any children.' Felicity raised her mug to her lips. It had just been a casual query on Joe's part, obviously running on from the comment about what children looked like when they were asleep. It wasn't really a personal question so why had it felt so personal? She was thirty-five years old, after all. Most women her age had children. Even women who worked full time in a demanding job such as hers.

'That's a shame.'

The disappointment in Joe's tone was sincere enough to make the exchange a lot more personal. Hurtful, even. Of course it was a shame. Felicity loved children. She would dearly love to have some of her own but the chances of that happening were getting fainter with every passing year. It was a reminder that Felicity didn't need rubbed in. Especially coming from a particularly attractive man who was already well sorted with a wife and family of his own.

'Which is more disappointing—that I'm not married or that I don't have children?'

Joe's glance was quizzical. Was he aware that the cool tone might reveal personal offence rather than disinterest? The hint of apology in his smile suggested a sensitivity that Felicity would have preferred not to have had confirmed.

'It's a shame you don't have children. I thought you might be able to help me with a small domestic crisis. No.' Joe's face took on a comically agonised expression as he sighed dramatically. 'Make that a very large domestic crisis. Huge, even.'

Felicity laughed. Her amusement was partly due to Joe's acting ability. It was also tinged with relief that he'd backed off from such a sensitive topic concerning herself. What would she have said if he'd told her she'd make a great mother or asked whether she wanted children in the future? That she'd never managed to attract anybody she would be remotely interested in having children with?

'Why don't you tell me about it anyway?' Felicity said encouragingly. 'I might be able to help. I was a kid once.'

'You still are—just about.' Joe's glance was appraising. 'What are you, twenty-eight? Twenty-nine?' He shook his head. 'I can't believe you're a consultant already. Here I am at thirty-eight and I'm still hunting for a job.'

'I'm thirty-five, actually,' Felicity informed him. She smiled. 'But I have an excellent long-term memory. What's the problem?'

'It's my daughter. Sam,' Joe reminded Felicity unnecessarily. He paused and sighed heavily again, this time with obvious sincerity. 'She's turning five in a couple of weeks and I'm informed that this is a very important occasion.'

'It is a biggie,' Felicity agreed. 'Starting school and so on. Quite a milestone.'

'Mmm.' Joe was staring into his coffee-mug. 'The thing is, I've offered to arrange the birthday party.' He glanced up, chewing the inside of his cheek thoughtfully. 'Actually, I've *insisted* on arranging the birthday party. All by myself.' The shy smile was appealing. 'It's my first time.' The smile turned into a lopsided grin. 'I'm a virgin party arranger.'

Oh, help! Felicity swallowed hard. The sexual connotations of the adjective were impossible to ignore. Teamed with that killer smile and the appeal in those brown eyes, Felicity knew she was in serious danger of losing her composure if not her morals. She reminded herself sternly of the existence of Joe's wife and children, but it wasn't helping as much as it usually did. Felicity tried harder.

'You won't need to do it all by yourself,' she said reassuringly. 'I'm sure your wife won't let you suffer that much.'

'Wife?' Joe's tone was bewildered. 'I haven't got a wife. What makes you think I have?'

'I saw her.' Felicity wasn't going to be deceived no matter how tempting the prospect might be. 'The blonde woman who came to collect Sam from Emergency the day she broke her arm.'

'That was Dayna.' Joe was staring at Felicity. 'She's not my wife. I haven't got a wife.'

The repetition was unsatisfactory. 'Who is Dayna, then?' Probably an ex-wife, Felicity decided. There was no reason for Joe to look quite so startled. It had been an obvious assumption to make on her part. He was nodding now as though in agreement.

'Dayna is Sam's aunt. My sister-in-law. Or, more correctly, my ex-sister-in-law, I guess.'

'Ah. You're divorced, then?' It was Felicity's turn to nod. That might explain the animosity in the conversation she'd overheard concerning Samantha's injury.

'No, I'm not divorced.' Joe took a deep breath. He was watching Felicity carefully. She returned the look unblinkingly, listening.

'My wife, Catherine, had a car accident when she was about four months' pregnant with Sam. She sustained a high cervical injury that was badly mismanaged at the accident scene.'

Felicity's coffee was forgotten. Her mind was drawn instantly back to her first meeting with Joe.

So, he'd had a personal agenda at the scene which she'd had no inkling of.

'I wasn't there,' Joe continued quietly. 'But Catherine knew enough not to try and move with the pain she had in her neck. She had no neurological symptoms to start with—no paralysis or paresthesia. I assume that her spinal cord was intact at that point. The lesion was incomplete until some well-meaning member of the public insisted on dragging her out of the car, thinking that there was a fire risk.'

Felicity's breath escaped in an appalled groan. 'Oh, no!' She shook her head. No wonder Joe had seemed over the top, the way he'd taken command of the accident scene at the building site. He'd had every reason to be.

'She actually felt the bone in her neck snap,' Joe said softly. 'Instantaneous and total paralysis. If the same person who dragged her out hadn't known how to keep her breathing until the ambulance arrived, I wouldn't have Sam around today.'

'So Catherine died?' Felicity queried gently. She frowned. Hadn't Joe said she'd been four months pregnant? That was far too early for a baby to survive a premature birth.

'Not until nearly a year later,' Joe responded heavily. 'She was kept alive on a ventilator. The birth was done by Caesarean section at about twenty-eight weeks. It was touch and go for Sam for a while but she pulled through and hasn't shown any adverse effects, thank God.'

There was a moment's silence.

'That must have been so hard, Joe,' Felicity said softly. 'Especially for you—knowing how different the outcome might have been if someone had known what they were doing at the time of the accident.'

'It was worse than you think. I wasn't in neuro-surgery then. I initially trained as an orthopaedic surgeon. At the time of Catherine's accident I was working in the specialist spinal unit in Wellington. I'd become interested in the work of a neurosurgeon who worked with the orthopaedic team that spe-cialised in rehabilitative surgery for complications of paralysis. It seemed like a new direction I could take after her death so I went to the States for post-graduate training. That's why I'm still a registrar at the ripe old age of thirty-eight.'

Felicity jumped at the sound of the pager but it wasn't her or Joe being summoned. Colin stirred in the depths of the armchair in the corner and then pushed himself to his feet with a groan. As he stum-bled away Felicity realised that the rest of the staff-room had emptied without her having been aware of the exodus, so intent had she been on her conver-sation with Joe. Things must be getting busier in the department again but she hoped she might have a few more minutes. Felicity didn't want to stop talking to Joe just yet.

'How did Sam enjoy living in the States?'

'She didn't come with me.' Joe frowned. 'I wanted to take her but Dayna persuaded me it would be better for Sam to stay with her.' The look Joe gave Felicity contained a mixture of emotions. Clearly he had regretted the decision. Maybe he was even ashamed of having made it.

'Dayna is Catherine's sister,' he explained. 'She's married to Nigel who is some sort of computer genius with a large company. They move around every two or three years but they were living in Wellington at the time of the accident—not far from Catherine and me, in fact. They were both very supportive. I couldn't have managed to look after Sam when she came home if it hadn't been for Dayna's help, and she had two young boys of her own to care for as well.' He cleared his throat. 'Dayna has a fairly strong personality.'

Felicity smiled at the diplomatic comment. 'I noticed,' she said.

'She can be very determined to get what she wants and she decided that she wanted to raise her niece, at least for a year or two. I think she'd always wanted a daughter but Nigel hadn't been keen on any more children after the boys.'

'He didn't mind having Sam, then?'

'He didn't have much choice.' Joe smiled wryly. 'It's a strong man that can stand up to Dayna. I wasn't a strong man at the time. On top of Catherine's accident and hospitalisation and death, I was struggling to cope with caring for a tiny baby. I needed to get away from my position at the spinal unit and the notion of retraining seemed like a way to start putting my life back together. Dayna persuaded me to get settled in a new country before taking Sam to live with me.' He shook his head. 'Every time I rang or came back to visit there were new reasons why it wasn't quite the right time to reclaim my daughter. She was settled in Christchurch and she had extended her family by including grandparents. They're my parents,' Joe explained. 'I actually grew up in Christchurch myself. Anyway, there were lots of other reasons. She had friends at kindergarten. Girls need a mother. She might stifle a new relationship I could find.'

'Did you?' Felicity couldn't help the question popping out.

'Did I what?'

'Find a new relationship?'

'Good grief, that was the last thing on my mind. I hadn't even considered looking. I concentrated on my training with the aim of getting established and getting my daughter back again. I didn't quite realise how much time it was taking until Dayna told me they were due for another move. Australia this time. That's why I came back to New Zealand. Dayna's excuses about not disrupting Sam's life by moving her to a new country don't hold water any more. And I knew that if I didn't reclaim Sam now I might lose her for ever.'

'So you're planning to take her back to the States?'

'No. It's not a place I want to bring up a child. I've moved here permanently.' Joe smiled without amusement. 'I can even use some of Dayna's arguments for my own case. Sam is settled here. It's her home. She has friends and grandparents and she'll have a father.'

'So Sam is living with you now?'

'Not quite.' Joe frowned. 'I couldn't stay with my parents because they've moved into a small unit in a retirement village. Their health isn't great now. I'm in a flat while I'm house-hunting and it's not really suitable for a child. And I want to give everybody a bit of time to get used to the idea so things don't turn unpleasant. Dayna isn't going to give in easily. At the moment she's engaged in a campaign to convince me, and probably Sam, that I'm not the best parent material.'

'How can she do that?'

'Doesn't seem to be difficult.' Joe's grin was embarrassed. 'Seems like I have a knack of causing minor disasters. Like letting Sam ruin a new dress by spilling raspberry drink all over it. Like losing the doll Dayna had given her for Christmas last year, and being late when I promised to turn up. She was furious when I was late the day I stopped to help with that accident.'

Felicity's eyebrows had been rising steadily. 'They're hardly major crimes.'

'She broke her arm the first time I took her to the park. That was a biggie.'

'Hmm. I can see that might have been more difficult to handle. But hadn't one of her sons had the same injury a while back?'

'How on earth did you know that?'

'I overheard her telling you off,' Felicity confessed. She grinned. 'Maybe that's why I thought she was your wife.'

Joe's look was speculative. 'I think we might discuss your peculiar views on marriage another time. So far you haven't been much help with my crisis.'

'I haven't had the chance,' Felicity protested through a smile. The thought of another personal discussion with Joe was very appealing. 'You distracted me.'

'I was giving you background,' Joe amended sternly. 'So you realise what's at stake here. I've set myself up for a complete failure by taking on this birthday party. Not only will Dayna have another

disaster to add to the list of reasons why I'm not cut
out to be a solo parent but Sam will be disappointed
and might agree with her.'

'Ah. So you not only want to deliver the party,
you want to do it well enough to give Sam the time
of her life and stun Dayna into silence—at least temporarily.'

'Easy.' Joe grinned. Then he groaned. 'Not!'

'It might not be impossible, however. All you
need is expert advice. Or at least plenty of support
from someone who knows enough about kids' parties to be able to assist you.'

'I can't ask Dayna and I don't know anyone else
like that.'

'Yes, you do.'

'Who?'

'Me.' Felicity smiled. 'My friends have been busy
producing babies and having parties for the last ten
years. I've picked up a few clues along the way
purely through osmosis.'

'And you'd help?' Joe's smile was dubious.

'Of course. It sounds like fun.'

It sounded like a lot more than fun as far as
Felicity was concerned. She had no intention of ad-
mitting anything but she owed Joe some kind of
apology for the assumptions she'd been making
about him in the last few weeks. She'd brushed off
every friendly approach he'd made, thinking he was

a married rat. What's more, she'd been expending a considerable amount of emotional energy keeping a lid on her supposedly inappropriate reactions to the man. Now she didn't need to any more.

Yes! Helping Joe to stage his daughter's birthday party was going to be more than fun.

It was going to be pretty damned exciting!

CHAPTER FIVE

THE opportunity was heaven-sent.

Joe had had no idea how much time and effort organising a five-year-old child's birthday party could entail. He sat in Felicity's office the following evening with a slightly stunned expression on his face.

'Why aren't you taking notes?' Felicity asked. 'You're never going to remember all this.'

'You're not wrong there,' Joe agreed. He pulled the booklet normally reserved for clinical notes from his pocket and flipped it open. 'Could we start at the beginning again, please, Fliss?'

'Decide on the date and time. The invitations will need to be sent out as soon as possible. The birthday falls on a Saturday, doesn't it?' Felicity checked the calendar on the wall behind her desk. 'Yes, it does. It's the second Saturday in September. That's good. We can make it a lunchtime party and the children won't get too tired. Are you on duty that day at all?'

'No. I requested it off a while back.'

'Great. I'm not on either. Now, you need to make a list of guests. Who are you planning to invite?'

'Dayna and Nigel and the boys will have to be

invited and my parents, although they probably won't stay very long. They're not in the best of health these days. And some kids around Sam's age, I guess.'

Felicity smiled. 'That might be a good idea. How many were you thinking of?'

'I've got no idea.' Joe looked thoughtful. 'Couldn't I just put a notice up at kindy and we'll see who turns up?'

'How many children go to Sam's kindergarten?'

'Maybe forty or fifty?'

Felicity laughed. 'We want a party, not a circus. Ask Sam who her special friends are. Narrow it down to ten at the most and find out whether she wants any boys to come.'

'Boys?' Joe looked alarmed. 'She's a bit young to be worrying about that sort of thing, isn't she?'

Felicity gave him a kind glance. 'It still makes a difference to what sort of party we have. Boys wouldn't like dressing up as fairies, for example, whereas a group of five-year-old girls would probably love it. Boys would be OK with clowns, though. Or pirates. Or ponies.'

'Ponies? Bit hard to dress up as a pony, isn't it?'

Felicity laughed again. 'Party ponies. One of my friends had them. They arrive in a float and the kids get to groom them and saddle them up and then have turns riding. Takes care of most of the entertainment so you don't have to rack your brains for games or deal with bored children.'

Joe shook his head. 'We can't do that.'

'What—deal with bored children? Speak for yourself, mate. I've had experience with dealing with major tantrums in Emergency. I always win.'

'I'm sure,' Joe said drily. 'I meant we can't have ponies.'

'Why not? Doesn't Sam like ponies?'

'She loves anything with fur that breathes, but it would be far too dangerous.'

'Nonsense.' Was Joe an over-protective parent? 'These are hand-picked ponies. They're as gentle as they come.'

'It's not the ponies I'm worried about. It's the traffic.'

'Traffic?'

'My flat's upstairs in a central city apartment block. The only place they could go riding is on the footpath down the one-way system. The traffic is always heavy.'

'No problem. We can have the party at my place.'

Joe blinked. This was great. Excellent, in fact. He was going to find out where Felicity lived.

'I've got a couple of acres of garden but I'm right on the edge of town so it's not too far for anyone to travel.'

'Sounds fantastic.' Joe was cautiously enthusiastic. 'Are you sure you don't mind?'

'I wouldn't offer if I did. I've got a huge old house that's been pretty empty and too quiet since my dad died last year. It'll be fun having a bunch of kids running around and making some noise.' Felicity smiled. 'So, what do you think? Shall we go for the ponies?'

'What were the other options again?'

'You could have the party catered for in a fast-food restaurant if you want it to be no effort at all.'

Joe shook his head. 'That certainly wouldn't impress Dayna. Anyone could do that.'

'You could hire a clown or a magician or even a bouncy castle.'

'What's a bouncy castle?'

'A huge blow-up toy that kids hurl themselves around in and bounce on. It's a good idea to confine the bouncing to before they have anything to eat, though.'

'Forget the castle,' Joe said hurriedly. 'I quite liked that fairy idea. Sam loves dressing up.'

'Fairies are good.'

Joe grinned. 'Could we do fairies *and* ponies?'

Felicity returned the smile. 'Why not? We want to blow Dayna's socks off here, don't we?'

'Absolutely.'

'OK. Fairies *and* ponies it is. Make a note.'

Joe scribbled rapidly and then closed his note-book. 'Fantastic. Thanks, Fliss.' He glanced at his watch and stood up. 'My shift starts in five minutes and you're probably busy so I'd better get out of your hair.'

'Sit down,' Felicity suggested firmly. 'We haven't even started your list properly yet.'

'What do you mean?'

'We need to discuss costumes and food and dec-orations. Make some shopping lists. What about Sam's birthday present? What games will we plan for and what will we put in the goodie bags for the children to take home? Who's going to blow up all the balloons and bake the cake? I can't do all this by myself, you know, Joe. I offered to help, not take over.'

'Of course not. Whew!' Joe sat down, opened his notebook again and tried to look thoughtfully atten-tive rather than totally delighted. They were going to have to do a lot of talking over the next two weeks. They might need to go shopping together. They would definitely need some time at Felicity's house to set up the decorations. And Felicity was looking positively enthusiastic about the prospect. This was good. Excellent, in fact.

Felicity thoroughly enjoyed the novelty of the build-up to Samantha's party. And consultant Gareth

Harvey enjoyed the snatches of the odd conversations he heard in the emergency department over the next two weeks. Sometimes they started off quite normally.

'So what did you think about Mr Stephens?' Felicity had intercepted Joe as he'd emerged from Resus 4.

'You're quite right about the abnormalities on the CT scan. It's a small lesion but enough to explain the seizure. I've started him on an anticonvulsant and admitted him for further investigations. I'd say he'll be heading for surgery pretty soon. Let's hope it's not something malignant, for his sake.'

'Mmm.' Felicity had seemed satisfied with the hand-over of her patient. 'And what did you decide about the fairies? Just wings and wands or shall we go the whole hog and have dresses?'

To Gareth's astonishment, Joe had seemed to give the question serious consideration.

'Just wings and wands, I guess.'

'We could do sparkly headbands and I've found a can of glitter spray.' Felicity had looked very pleased with herself. 'Non-toxic. Looks just like fairy dust to me.' Then she'd noticed the strange look she'd been receiving from Gareth and had cleared her throat. 'What dose of phenytoin did you say you started Mr Stephens on, Joe?'

There were other times when Gareth wondered

whether Joe had come to the emergency department to see a patient at all. On one occasion he was carrying a large paper bag that Felicity seemed very keen to peer into.

'Oh, good. You've got lots of different colours. We don't want to go too feminine and stick to pink. Were they hard to find?'

'Not at all. I went to that shop you told me about. They can do almost everything we need.'

The visits became more frequent during the second week. Notes were seen to be compared and exchanged.

'Don't forget the carrots,' Felicity reminded Joe, who wrote down the strange instruction.

'Did we decide on strawberry or chocolate?' he countered.

'Chocolate,' Felicity said firmly. 'I don't do strawberry.'

The chocolate proved to be enough of a challenge. On the eve of the party, Felicity lifted the spoon in the bowl of icing she was preparing. She watched the large drips forming and sighed.

'It doesn't seem to make any difference how much icing sugar I put in. It's still too runny.'

Joe looked up from a rainbow sea of coloured balloons covering the floor of the farmhouse kitchen. He smiled confidently. 'It'll taste great. Don't worry about it.' Joe's smile was only partly due to the encouragement he was imparting. He was enjoying himself immensely. Here he was, in Felicity's house. He was seeing her away from a professional environment for the first time and she looked great—snug-fitting jeans, a soft, warm jersey and her long hair flowing loose over her shoulders. He had resisted more than one urge to bury his hands in the rich, brown tresses to see if it felt as silky as it looked.

'Maybe it'll set in the fridge overnight.' Felicity still looked worried. 'I haven't got time to make any more. We need to finish the decorations and lay out the treasure hunt.'

'How did you get on with the clues?'

'I thought you were doing the clues.' Felicity groaned. 'I think I need a glass of wine.'

An hour later, the bottle was almost empty and Felicity and Joe sat at the kitchen table, laughing helplessly.

'OK, then. What about this—to lead to the potting shed? "A little house all dark and scary. The spiders have gone to make room for a fairy."'

'Terrible!' Joe pronounced.

'No worse than yours.' Felicity dived on a scrap of paper. '"Find where this is and you'll be in luck,"' she quoted. '"There's feathers in here but they're not off a duck."'

'What's wrong with that? You said you had a hen-house.'

'Yes, but there aren't any hens around. Or feathers. We haven't kept any poultry since I was about Sam's age.'

'Have you always lived here?'

'I left home when I went to medical school. I came back a few years ago after Mum died and Dad got sick. It's a bit silly living here all by myself but I can't bring myself to sell the property just yet.'

'I can understand that. It's a beautiful house.' It had still been daylight when Joe had arrived and he'd been enchanted by the rambling, two-storeyed villa. The verandah was framed by an ancient wisteria vine that was getting ready to burst into spring blossom. The overgrown garden surrounded by impressively large, old trees was a perfect setting for the house.

'It's too big, really and the garden is turning into a wilderness.' Felicity hoped that Joe wouldn't hear the echoes of loneliness in her words. She smiled brightly. 'Come on, we'll find some torches and go exploring. We need to hide the clues.' Felicity picked up the bag of chocolate money. 'We'll put the treasure in the hen-house. That way they'll be too excited to notice there aren't any feathers.'

It was dark and cold outside but setting out the treasure hunt was fun and the frost promised the likelihood of a fine day for the party. Felicity was looking forward to the event but was sorry it would all be over by this time tomorrow. The organisation had been a real joy. Would Joe be so keen to see her when there wasn't such an important incentive for her company? Tonight was the first time they had been together outside the hospital environment. Felicity had entertained hopes that the change might give them a chance to get closer, but there had been too much to do and now it was late and Joe was preparing to leave.

He took a final look at the decorations and the party food arranged on the bench. A pile of tulle wings, wands and sparkly headbands was waiting by the front door for when the children arrived. Another pile of goodie bags was hiding discreetly under a hall table for when the children left to go home.

'You've gone to so much trouble over this,' Joe told Felicity. 'I can't thank you enough.'

'It's been a pleasure,' Felicity responded. She was caught by the appreciative look she was receiving. 'I've really enjoyed it,' she added softly.

Joe looked as though he wanted to kiss her. Felicity wanted Joe to kiss her. She *really* wanted it. Maybe *she* should kiss *him*? Felicity almost moved forward but stopped herself abruptly. She'd never made the first move in a situation like this and

Joe was looking at her rather oddly. Maybe her embarrassment was contagious.

'I'd better go. See you tomorrow, Fliss.'

'OK. And don't worry, Joe. The party will be great.'

Joe wasn't worried. Even if the party was a total disaster it was going to be great. Joe took a very deep breath as he eased himself behind the wheel of his car. Hell, that must have been the hardest thing he'd ever done in his life, not kissing Felicity at the door. The wild notion of sweeping all five feet ten or so of her into his arms and running up the stairs to find her bedroom had been almost more than he'd been able to control. For a split second he'd even thought that Felicity might welcome the move. She must have caught at least the gist of his thoughts. She'd looked suddenly...what? Unsure? Embarrassed? Had she been wondering how she could deter him without causing offence? Joe had somehow found the strength not to risk discovering that Felicity wasn't ready for a kiss.

The last two weeks had revealed just how strongly Joe felt about this woman. Not only did she hold down a demanding job and cope superbly with whatever challenges the emergency department could throw at her, she could find the time and energy to throw herself wholeheartedly into helping a friend. And they *were* friends now. She appeared to enjoy his company as much as he did hers. This party-planning business had been a real eye-opener. How else could he have discovered the delightful scope of Felicity's imagination? Her willingness to tackle new ventures? Her generosity and sense of humour?

Joe was well and truly head over heels in love with Felicity now, and this was far, far too important to risk by trying to take the relationship to a more intimate level before he knew for sure that was what Felicity *really* wanted. But Joe had the feeling that he might find out before too long. He drove off into the night enveloped by the most exciting sense of anticipation he had ever known. This party wasn't just going to be great. It could possibly be the best thing that had ever happened to him.

'Happy birthday, Sam.'

Samantha pulled the wrapping from the small parcel. 'A pencil case,' she announced with delight. 'Look, Daddy. It's got felt-tips and a ruler and everything!'

'Just right for school. Wasn't Fliss clever to think of that?'

Samantha nodded. 'Daddy gave me a backpack,' she informed Felicity. 'The pencil case will fit inside.'

'I hope so.' Felicity smiled. 'Your friends will be

arriving for the party before too long, Sam. Do you want to put your wings on now?'

'No. I want to play with Rusty.'

The feathered tail thumped at the sound of his name. The old red dog moved closer to Samantha and the small girl wrapped her arms around his neck and kissed his nose enthusiastically.

'Can I have a dog, Daddy? Just like Rusty?'

'One day, Sam.' Joe reached out and stroked his daughter's curls. Felicity smiled. What a change from the last time she had seen these two together. The awkwardness had gone and there could be no mistaking the close bond between parent and child.

'When?'

'When I find us a house of our own.'

'Mum says I'm going to live in Australia with her and Uncle Nigel and the boys.'

'Does she, now?' Samantha didn't see the spark of anger in her father's face as she ran off to find the ball that Rusty had no intention of fetching. The dog followed her happily nonetheless.

'She had no right to tell Sam that.' Joe shook his head. 'I've got to do something about this situation.'

'When are they planning to move?'

'Not before the end of the year.'

'Then there's plenty of time. Look, is that Dayna's car coming up the driveway now?'

'Mmm.' Joe nodded towards the second car. 'And

that's my parents. I hope Mum isn't driving. Her eyesight is really failing now thanks to her diabetes.'

Felicity could hear the despondency in Joe's tone. She touched his arm lightly. 'Don't let it spoil today, Joe. For you or Sam. The closer you and Sam become the easier it will all be. You need to get settled with a place to live and show Dayna and Nigel how prepared you are to cope with raising Sam. She belongs with you and I'm sure Dayna understands that. She can't be planning to be too difficult about letting her go.'

'You don't know Dayna.' He caught Felicity's eye. 'But you soon will. Let's go and say hello to everybody.'

Felicity got to know Dayna a lot better over the next half-hour before the party guests arrived. Dayna was immaculately dressed in a slim-fitting dress with a matching tailored jacket. Her blonde shoulder-length bob curved under at the bottom and Felicity couldn't detect a single hair that was not co-operating with the elegant style. She would rather have spent the time with Joe's parents, who were a very likable elderly couple, but Dayna insisted on a tour of the house and garden.

'So how did Joe manage to persuade you to have Samantha's party here?'

'I offered,' Felicity said pleasantly. 'I didn't need any persuasion at all.'

Dayna paused at the top of the sweeping staircase. 'I wouldn't like to dust a house this size.'

'Neither would I.' Felicity grinned. 'That's why you can write your name on most of the furniture.'

'Do you have a gardener?' Dayna peered through the lead-lighted window on the landing.

'No.'

'I don't know how you cope. That's an enormous garden.'

'I don't,' Felicity said cheerfully. 'Wait until you see all the weeds.'

Dayna eyed the trays of pizza, fairy bread, tiny sausage rolls and fruit kebabs as they passed through the kitchen. 'What caterers did you use for the food?'

'We've done it all ourselves.' Joe's proud tone floated in from the adjacent living area. 'Except for the ponies.'

'Ponies?' Dayna sounded distinctly put out. 'That's a bit over the top isn't it?' She noticed the cups of tea Joe had provided for his parents. 'I could do with one of those,' she announced. 'Or preferably a glass of red wine.'

'I'll get one for you.' Joe caught Felicity's gaze as he walked past into the kitchen. They didn't need to share a smile. They knew exactly how much they would enjoy demonstrating just how well Joe could organise a birthday party.

'Don't kiss that dog, Samantha,' Dayna ordered. 'Dogs have germs.'

Dayna's husband, Nigel, and the two boys faded into the background along with the other adults as small girls began arriving. Fairy wings were donned, wands began waving enthusiastically and Felicity sprayed fairy dust onto hair and clothes.

'It's non-toxic,' she assured Dayna. 'And it washes out of fabric.'

'*Fairies!*' Fourteen-year-old Andrew looked disgusted. Ten-year-old Scott mirrored his expression.

'Do you have a PlayStation?' he demanded.

'No. Why don't you come on the treasure hunt instead?'

'You can play the games on my mobile,' Nigel told his sons. 'Just as soon as I've made a few calls.'

It was Joe and Felicity that led the tribe of excited fairies around the garden on the treasure hunt, Rusty following at a safe distance from the waving wands. It was Joe and Felicity that helped patiently lead the two Shetland ponies with their winged mounts up and down the long driveway, keeping impatient fairies entertained as they waited their turns.

Joe's parents stood nearby, beaming at Samantha at every opportunity. Dayna and Nigel shared a bottle of red wine sitting on the terrace. The two boys failed to share the cellphone and had it confiscated. They sat sullenly until the food was provided.

'Just as well we made heaps,' Felicity whispered to Joe. 'I can't believe how many sausage rolls Scott has managed to eat.'

Dayna might not have believed the quantity either had her son not provided the evidence.

'It really doesn't matter,' Felicity assured her. 'Someone always gets sick at a birthday party.'

'Even without bouncy castles.' Joe grinned. Dayna looked at him blankly and then frowned.

'I just hope no one else gets sick. It could be food poisoning.'

'Not likely.' Joe sounded firm. 'I think you should take Scott home, though, Dayna. He's not looking very happy.'

'We'll wait for the end of the party. Then we can take Samantha with us.'

'She's staying with me tonight. It's a weekend and I'm not on call.'

Dayna opened her mouth, clearly ready to suggest a new arrangement. The look that passed between Joe and Nigel prompted her husband to step in.

'It's time we went home, Dayna. Joe can bring Sam back when he's ready. Let's go and wish her happy birthday again and say goodbye.'

'We must go too, son,' Joe's father said. 'Your mum's looking pretty tired.' He patted Joe on the shoulder. 'You've done a wonderful job with this party. Sam looks very happy.'

Samantha continued to look very happy. When the last of the sticky chocolate icing had been wiped from many little fingers, the gifts from the guests were unwrapped. Parents arrived to collect the children at the appointed time and suddenly it was over. Joe and Felicity found themselves alone with one tired but still happy little fairy.

'I'd better take her home.'

'Do you have to? Right now, I mean? I was going to make us a coffee.'

'She's pretty tired.'

'She could have a sleep here. I've got spare beds made up.' Felicity used the main bedroom of the house these days but her childhood bedroom would still be an inviting place for a small girl. 'Would you like to see the room I had when I was your age, Sam?'

'Can Rusty come too?'

'Of course.'

Samantha loved the room, with the attic-type angles to the ceiling and the paned window that overlooked the orchard at the back of the house. Daylight had faded completely by the time they could persuade her away from the treasures to be found in an old toybox and coax her into bed.

'We need to take your wings off, sweetheart.'

'Why? I like being a fairy.'

'Well, they won't be very comfortable and they

might get bent. Look, we'll put them on the end of the bed and Rusty can look after them for you.'

'OK.'

The headband and wand stayed with the wings but the fairy dust was still in Samantha's curls as she put her head on the pillow and fell asleep almost instantly. Joe and Felicity went downstairs to the kitchen. The large red dog had no intention of leaving his post beside the bed.

Felicity sat quietly at the end of the old, scrubbed kitchen table. Joe placed a mug of coffee in front of her and sat down to one side.

'I should really clean this lot up.' Felicity eyed the debris scattered on the table before them. The birthday cake had been on a platter that was lying between her and Joe on the corner of the table. All that remained were a few crumbs and the five half-burnt candles dotted inside a frame of chocolate icing that had flowed out from the edges of the cake. Being refrigerated overnight hadn't been enough to solve the runny icing problem.

'Cleaning up can wait,' Joe said. 'I'll help you with that. Right now I want a few minutes to gloat and to tell you what a fantastic job you did.'

'*We* did.'

'I wouldn't have had a hope of doing a single part

of it without you. Now I'm a hero as far as Sam's concerned.'

'I suspect you always have been. Parenting isn't just about giving great parties, you know. They only become happy memories if the underlying relationship is sound.'

Joe nodded. 'The celebrations are the icing on the cake.'

'Speaking of which, that's one thing I didn't do very well at all.' Idly, Felicity traced her forefinger through a dollop of the chocolate icing on the edge of the platter. 'It was far too soft. I'll have to watch that next time.' She licked the icing off her finger. 'Tastes good, though.'

Felicity glanced up at Joe as she delivered the verdict. The gaze from the brown eyes fastened on her face made her acutely aware of the effect her action had had. The heat in Joe's eyes instantly ignited the flame of the desire Felicity realised had been building for weeks now. Perhaps ever since she had first met him. Silently and deliberately, Felicity traced her finger through the chocolate for a second time before slowly raising it to her lips, her gaze never leaving Joe's. Her hand was caught well before it made contact. The chocolate-covered finger touched Joe's lips rather than her own. His mouth closed softly around the digit and Felicity felt the firm caress of his tongue as he sucked the icing clear.

'You're right,' Joe murmured eventually. 'It tastes very good.'

Felicity couldn't say a word. She was melting. Never in her life had she experienced such intense physical desire, and the effect was immobilising. She could only watch, still stunned, as Joe placed her hand back on the table and used his own finger to scoop up another droplet of icing. He painted the soft chocolate on her lower lip. Felicity's breath caught and held as he bent his head towards hers.

The kiss tasted of chocolate. It smelt of chocolate. It was as warm and deep as chocolate but it was far, far more exciting than chocolate could ever hope to be. Felicity felt her head being cradled, her mouth angled to allow better access for Joe's thorough exploration of her lips and tongue. Her own hands moved to touch Joe's body. To hold him closer and prevent the kiss from ending too soon.

It had to end and it felt far too soon. Joe looked as stunned as Felicity had felt so many minutes ago now. Felicity smiled.

'I think,' she said slowly, 'that I might always make my icing a bit too soft.'

'I think that's a very good thought.' Joe had to clear his throat.

Felicity wanted another kiss. She wanted a lot

more than another kiss but she felt suddenly shy. Maybe Joe would think she was pushy if she made the next move.

'Maybe I'd better get on with this clearing up,' she suggested hesitantly.

'That's not a good thought,' Joe told her. 'I have a much better one.'

'Do you?' Felicity tried not to sound too eager. 'What's that?'

'I think we should test that icing a bit more.' Joe's gaze was burning her now. 'In bed,' he added softly. 'Sam will sleep for hours. She probably won't wake up until morning even when I carry her out to the car to go home.'

'The icing might be kind of messy.' Felicity's difficulty in catching her breath made it hard to speak.

Joe smiled. 'I'm sure you taste lovely without it,' he said seriously. His smile was an irresistible invitation. 'Shall I find out?'

Felicity held out her hand by way of response. She glanced down at the cake platter as Joe led her away from the table. They had no need of the chocolate icing any more.

No need at all.

CHAPTER SIX

'GOOD grief!'

The reaction to the initial sight of the traumatic injury was not the most professional but Felicity murmured her whole-hearted agreement.

'I'm so glad you're on duty, Joe. We couldn't decide whether to call in Orthopaedics first or Neurosurgery or Vascular Surgery. With you we get all three rolled into one.' She smiled wryly. 'It's crowded enough in here already. We've even had the photography department excited.'

'I'm not surprised. Looks more like a shark attack than a close encounter with a concrete mixer. How old is David?'

'Twenty-seven.'

'How stable is he?' Joe was still making a careful visual inspection of the mangled lower arm of the unconscious young man occupying the trauma room bed.

Felicity's report on the patient's condition revealed how serious his condition had been on arrival. The blood loss had been severe enough to be immediately life-threatening. David's blood pressure had been too low to record and his level of consciousness very low. He had been intubated to try and improve his oxygenation level but it was still low enough to be giving concern. Volume replacement with a blood transfusion was needed as soon as the cross-matching was completed. Joe was now evaluating the torn muscles and broken bones. Blood was still oozing steadily from multiple sites.

'Direct pressure hasn't been enough to control the haemorrhage completely even with elevation,' Felicity told him. 'I didn't want to put a tourniquet on in case the limb is salvageable. C-spine and chest were clear on X-ray,' she added. 'And the secondary survey hasn't shown any other major injuries.'

Joe caught Felicity's eye. He raised an eyebrow. 'I think this one might be quite enough.'

'It's a mess, isn't it? The little finger was torn off completely. It's in a bag in iced water over there.'

'The bone could be useful for grafting. We'll take it up to Theatre with us.'

'Do you think there's a chance he'll keep his arm?'

'We'll do our best. I want to get it thoroughly cleaned up and debrided and have a better look.' Joe nodded at the house surgeon standing beside him. 'You can put that pressure dressing back on again. The less exposure this gets the better as far as infection goes.' He turned back to Felicity. 'What prophylactic antibiotics have you started?'

'Cephalosporin and gentamicin. He's had a tetanus booster as well.'

'Good.' Joe moved towards the X-ray viewing screens. 'The head of the radius is a mess,' he commented. 'But the elbow is salvageable. The fingers aren't great and there's not much left of the midradial shaft, is there?'

'Can it be grafted?'

'Depends on how many bone fragments are available.' Joe's smile was rather grim. 'And how much cement we've got. Reducing the fractures isn't the main problem, though. There's the tendons, nerves and blood supply to get back together well enough to provide some function. It's going to be a long job.'

'I'd love to watch,' Felicity told him. 'I was actually going off duty when David came in. Is it going to be too crowded in Theatre for an extra?'

'Not if the extra is you.' Joe's face softened for a brief moment before he pulled the X-rays clear of the screens. 'Let's go,' he suggested. 'They'll be ready for us upstairs.'

Joe had been correct in his estimation of the lengthy nature of the surgery. And Felicity had been justified in querying how crowded the operating theatre would be. Surgeons from several different specialties became involved in the attempt to save David Carr's arm and hand but it was Joe who did most of the work. Screws, wires and pins were used to align fractured bones. Muscles, tendons and blood vessels were meticulously matched and joined. He used an operating microscope to tackle the repair of major nerves.

Felicity was amazed to look at the clock and find that four hours had passed. She had been fascinated by the surgery and more impressed than ever by Joe. It had been like revisiting an anatomy lecture at medical school, listening to Joe's explanations of what he was trying to do. Muscles such as the extensor carpi radialis longus and the palmar aponeurosis. Tendons like the abductor pollius brevis, and nerves like the posterior interosseous. Not only could Joe name them, he could locate them in an arm that looked nothing like nature had intended. He had to locate both ends of the anatomical structures and then rejoin them with surgical techniques that looked incredibly intricate. Felicity was more than impressed. She was blown away by the evident skill of this man.

And that was only one aspect of Joe that had Felicity captivated. It had been two weeks since Samantha's birthday party. Two weeks in which she and Joe had become lovers and discovered a depth to their relationship that had left Felicity stunned by its significance. Joe seemed to feel the same way. Not a day had passed since the birthday party without some form of contact other than professional. Phone calls, coffee, a dinner together on one of the few nights they both had clear. A call from Joe's father had ended that evening prematurely. His mother hadn't been well and Joe had been obviously torn between the need to visit his parents and the desire to go home with Felicity.

'Go and see your mum,' Felicity had urged. 'Make sure she's OK. We've got all the time in the world. Your mum might not have.'

The previous Sunday they had taken Samantha out for the day and the Petersens had stayed late again, but this week had been a heavy one for Joe and Felicity and they had only managed an hour or two together on Wednesday evening before Joe had gone to work. Felicity had visited his flat for the first time and she could understand why Joe was keen to find somewhere else to live with his daughter.

The flat was on a busy main road. The building itself lacked any character and the long two-storeyed structure looked like motel units. Joe's flat was on the second storey up a narrow iron staircase and along a walkway that rattled when the occupants of the next-door unit came and went. The windows of the sitting room and bedroom looked out onto the walkway and allowed little privacy unless the curtains were drawn.

'It's awful,' Joe apologised. 'But it's only temporary.' He handed Felicity a key. 'It's a spare key for the flat,' he told her. 'I'd like you to have it. Just in case you come to visit and I'm not home. You can come in and make yourself a coffee.'

Felicity hadn't offered Joe a key to her house. Not yet. But, then, she'd barely had the chance to talk to him since then. It was now the early hours of another Friday as Felicity watched the final work on David Carr's arm. She wanted to wait and talk to Joe. She wanted to suggest another outing for Samantha tomorrow. Maybe even another visit to her house.

Joe looked exhausted as he stripped off his gloves and mask. Dark stubble shadowed his lower face and the lines around his eyes had deepened noticeably. Felicity had to resist the urge to touch his cheek. To convey sympathy for his weariness but also to take pleasure in what she suspected would be an excitingly different texture to his skin. With other theatre staff still nearby she avoided any intimate touch other than eye contact. The smile on Joe's face by way of response chased much of the exhaustion away.

'How did you find that, Fliss? Any ambitions to become a neurosurgeon?'

'Are you kidding? I'd have enough trouble naming half those structures you were repairing.'

Felicity's tone became serious. 'That was absolutely amazing, Joe. You're extremely talented.'

'A lot of it is just being meticulous. And patient.' Joe's gaze roved over Felicity's face. 'You must be tired. You'd finished a full day before you even came in here. What's the time now?'

'Nearly one a.m. When do you finish your shift?'

Joe grinned. 'Over an hour ago. Can I buy you a coffee?'

'I'd love one.'

An all-night café not far from the hospital provided excellent cappuccinos. Joe and Felicity had finished their first cups by the time Joe had answered the questions Felicity still had about the surgery on David's arm. They ordered a second coffee.

'Are you working tomorrow?'

'Till five p.m.'

'Oh.' The disappointment in Felicity's tone was unmistakable. 'No outing for Sam, then.'

'I'm going to see her for dinner.' Joe looked at Felicity thoughtfully. 'Dayna's asked me to bring you along as well.'

'Did she?' Felicity was surprised.

'Sam told her about visiting your house again last weekend.'

Felicity bit her lip. 'At least she has no idea how late you stayed. She doesn't even wake up when you carry her out to the car.'

'I'm a bit worried about Dayna finding out we're more than friends.'

'Why? Wasn't one of her reasons for keeping Sam to give you the freedom to find another relationship?'

'Theoretically. The idea that I might be heading for something serious might seem a threat.'

Felicity was distracted from thinking about Dayna. A peculiar tingle was running through her body.

'Are you, Joe? Heading for something serious?'

'I hope so.' Joe reached out and caught one of Felicity's hands. 'I'm in love with you, Fliss. I never thought I'd ever feel so serious about anyone again in my life.'

The tingle was engulfed in a rush of emotion that made it difficult to speak in more than a whisper.

'I love you, too, Joe. I've never met anyone like you. I don't expect I ever will again.'

'I don't want to rush you. We haven't known each other very long.'

'Maybe we don't need to. I know how I feel, Joe. I never thought I could feel this strongly about someone.' Felicity smiled. 'I'm just sorry I spent all those weeks thinking you were an arrogant surgeon and an unfaithful husband. What a waste.'

'We'll make up for it.'

'OK.'

'Why don't we start making up for it right now?' Joe's fingers were weaving around Felicity's with a slow stroking motion. His gaze didn't waver from her eyes.

Felicity grinned. 'Bit public, isn't it?'

'Let's go home. Rusty must be missing you. He hasn't seen you all day.' The grip on Felicity's hand tightened. '*I'm* missing you and I've seen you three times today.'

It wasn't until much, much later as they lay still entwined in her bed that Felicity remembered the start of that conversation.

'What did you say when Dayna asked you to bring me to dinner?'

'I said I'd see if you were available.'

'Do you want me to be available?'

Joe planted a long kiss on Felicity's lips. 'Oh, yes,' he murmured. 'I want you to be available as often as possible.'

Felicity smiled. She curled up even closer within the circle of Joe's arms. 'I'm not talking about that. I'm trying to find out if you want me to come to dinner with you.'

'You might not enjoy it.'

'Why not? Is Dayna a really bad cook?'

Joe chuckled. 'Dayna's meals are perfect. It's just as well she's never tasted my cooking or she'd have a real reason to worry about Sam's future welfare.'

He kissed Felicity's neck and then sighed lightly. 'I'm just worried that getting involved in the complications I have with my family life might put you off me.'

'I'm already involved, Joe.'

'Dayna can get some strange ideas sometimes. I don't want Sam being used as a pawn.'

'Neither do I, but this is something that has to be sorted out, Joe. Sam is your daughter and she belongs with you. You're not going to sort this out by yourself so I may as well know what I'm up against. I want to come to the dinner.'

'OK. I'll pick you up as soon as I've finished work.'

'What time do you start?'

'Seven a.m.'

'Oh.' Felicity turned her head to kiss Joe's shoulder. 'You'd better get some sleep, then. It's awfully late.'

'I suppose I'd better. So had you.'

'I'm all right. I've got tomorrow off. I can sleep as late as I like.'

Joe's hand traced the length of Felicity's spine. 'Actually,' he whispered, 'I don't feel very sleepy at all right now.'

It was no wonder that Joe looked tired when he arrived to collect Felicity on Saturday evening.

'You should have had a lot more sleep than you did,' she told him.

'It was worth it.' Joe pulled Felicity into his arms and kissed her. 'Of course, we could go and have a bit of a lie-down now.'

'No, we couldn't.' Felicity grinned but her tone was nervous. 'Dayna's expecting us and I don't want to get off on the wrong foot by being late. I think I'm scared of her.'

'You have every reason to be,' Joe said unhelpfully.

Joe's gloomy prediction seemed misplaced when they arrived at the Jacksons' huge house set well up on the Cashmere hills overlooking Christchurch city. Dayna was very welcoming.

'Joe—how lovely to see you.' She stood on tiptoe to put her hands on Joe's shoulders, tilting her head to present her cheek for a kiss. Joe obliged.

'And...Felicity, isn't it?' Dayna turned a charming smile towards her other guest.

'Fliss,' Felicity corrected. 'I've never much liked Felicity.'

'Fliss! Fliss!' Samantha came running down the stairs. She was wearing flannelette pyjamas. Her fairy wings looked odd against the print of pink teddy bears. 'I drawed a picture for you at school,' Samantha told Felicity proudly. 'A picture of Rusty.'

'Did you?' Felicity sounded suitably impressed. 'I can't wait to see it.'

'Bedtime in five minutes, Samantha,' Dayna reminded her niece.

Felicity saw some of the joy fade from Joe's smile as he greeted his daughter. 'Surely she can stay up a little longer tonight. I've hardly seen her all week.'

'A little while longer,' Dayna conceded.

Felicity looked away. Was time with Samantha always rationed, with Dayna holding the power of decision? How had Joe allowed her to have such a hold on the situation?

'Will you read me a story, Daddy?'

'Of course I will, chicken.'

Felicity noticed the toy under Samantha's arm as she followed the others across an atrium into a formal lounge.

'Wow! Woof Woof Snowball *is* as white as Snow!' she exclaimed.

'He had a bath at Daddy's house.'

'It took days to get it properly dry, Joe. It should have gone to the dry-cleaner's or through the washing machine. Damp toys can grow fungus and cause asthma.'

'Really?' Joe avoided the opportunity to disagree. He walked towards an oak cabinet. 'Shall I get us all a drink?'

'Please. I'll have a Scotch.' Dayna sat down

gracefully on a leather armchair, looking perfectly in place in the elegant room.

'Fliss?'

'A white wine would be lovely, thanks, Joe.' Felicity glanced around her as she perched on a long leather couch. The huge room was divided by an arched beam at one end. A dining table could be seen set with a white linen cloth, candles and four place settings gleaming with silverware and crystal. So even the older children were not going to share the meal. Felicity took a long sip of her wine as Samantha scrambled onto the couch to sit beside her.

'I sleep on a couch at Daddy's house,' she told Felicity.

'Is it as slippery as this one?'

'No.' Samantha grinned. 'I'd fall off.' She eyed Felicity. 'Can I sleep in the bed at your house again? With Rusty?'

Felicity could feel the laser beam of Dayna's attention. Joe's hand paused in mid-air as he poured his own glass of wine.

'You *slept* at Felicity's house?' The calm interest fooled no one but Samantha. 'You didn't tell me about that, Samantha.'

'It was no big deal.' Joe sounded equally calm. 'Sam was a bit tired after the party. She had a nap while I helped Fliss clean up.' He crossed the room and joined Felicity and Samantha on the couch. 'Where's Nigel tonight?'

'Working late.' The ice rattled in Dayna's glass as she swirled her drink. 'As usual.'

'How's school been, Sam?' Joe's arm bent the fairy wings but Samantha didn't notice. She snuggled closer to her father. 'Do you still like it?'

'Mmm. It's fun.'

Felicity could feel that Dayna's observation of her had lost little of its intensity. Maybe she should have dressed up more but Joe hadn't warned her how up-market this house was or how formal the dinner was going to be. She had imagined a casual evening meal shared with the children. Now her jeans and soft woollen top looked as though she hadn't cared about the impression she was making, and her loose hair made her feel positively scruffy. Joe was still wearing the smart trousers and shirt he'd worn to work so he fitted in just fine. Felicity took another mouthful of her wine. Even if she'd dressed in her usual work style she couldn't have competed with the perfectly groomed look that Dayna's beige linen trousers and the cream silk shirt gave her. Felicity gave up worrying about it. It would be far more helpful if she put the emotional effort into trying to get on with Dayna.

'You've got a long way to go to take Sam to

school,' she said by way of opening a conversation. 'It's right over my side of town.'

'The boys go to St Christopher's.' Dayna named the exclusive private school that was also on the western side of the city near Felicity's property. 'It's just as easy to drop Samantha off at the same time and the school has a very good reputation.'

Felicity nodded. Joe and Samantha were engaged in a quiet discussion about the pet rabbits that belonged to the junior department of her school. Felicity searched for a new topic of conversation to fill the silence between herself and her hostess but it wasn't easy. What on earth could they have in common? Dayna finished her drink and rose to refill her glass.

'Joe, why don't you take Samantha upstairs and read her bedtime story? Nigel should be home by the time you've finished and we can eat dinner.'

'I want Fliss to come, too,' Samantha protested.

'Next time,' Dayna said firmly.

'Give Daddy the picture of Rusty that you drew,' Felicity told Samantha softly. 'Please? I really want to see it.'

'OK. 'Night, Fliss.'

'Goodnight, sweetheart.' It was automatic to reach out and touch Samantha's curls. Felicity hadn't expected the small arms to wind themselves around her neck and the freckled face to come close enough for an enthusiastic kiss. Samantha then held her arms out for Joe to pick her up. Dayna smiled a little tightly as she kissed her niece and watched the pair leave the room.

'She looks so much like Catherine,' she told Felicity. 'My sister. She was Joe's wife, you know.'

'Mmm. I know.' Felicity smiled sympathetically. Maybe this was an opportunity to make real contact with Dayna. 'I heard about the accident. It must have been a dreadful time for all of you.'

'It certainly was. I doubt that Joe will ever get over it.'

'He told me how much help you were to him.'

Dayna looked pleased. 'Did he?'

'He said he couldn't have coped without you. It must have been a lot of work, helping with a baby when you had young children yourself.'

'It was nothing I didn't want to do. Samantha's a part of my family.' Dayna gave Felicity a very direct look. 'She always will be.'

'Of course.' Was Dayna going to draw lines in the sand right now? If Dayna actually raised the topic of keeping Samantha Felicity knew instinctively that she would have to try and avoid revealing how much Joe had already confided in her. As far as Dayna was concerned, Felicity was very much an outsider. She finished her glass of wine. She had the feeling that any line of attack Dayna chose would be a lot more subtle than that, but the abrupt ending to their time alone together as the door opened to admit Nigel was something of a relief.

'Hello, darling.' Nigel was also presented with a cheek to kiss. 'Did you have a good day?'

'So-so. Hi, Fliss. How are you?' Nigel was pouring himself a drink already. 'That was a great birthday party.' He held up his glass. 'Cheers.'

'I thought the ponies were a bit much,' Dayna observed lightly. 'Nigel, Felicity's glass is empty.'

'Thanks.' Felicity handed over her glass. She smiled at Dayna. 'I really enjoyed having the ponies around. I had one of my own when I was Sam's age. It lived in the orchard at the back of the house.'

'You've got a nice spot there,' Nigel commented. 'It's farmland behind you, isn't it? Can't be built out, I guess.'

Felicity nodded. 'I've only got two acres but it seems a lot larger with the paddocks to look out on.'

'Do you own the house?' The query came from Dayna.

'Yes. It belonged to my parents but they're both dead now.'

'I'm sorry to hear that,' Nigel said. 'Were you an only child?'

'Yes.'

'Joe's looking for a house.' Dayna's tone suggested that the property might be what was attractive about Felicity. It was at that point that Felicity gave up trying to like Dayna. She also resolved not to let anything this woman might say get under her skin. She held onto that resolve through the melon entrée that Dayna served a short time later and well into the main course of the perfectly cooked rack of lamb and warm vegetable salad.

Nigel was an ally. Or, at least, he tried to be.

'So you're a consultant in the emergency department, Fliss? That's a very impressive achievement.' His admiration was sincere. 'Must be a tough job.'

'Especially for a woman,' Dayna added. She reached sideways to touch Joe's arm. 'Can I give you some more of this salad?'

'No, I'm fine, thanks.' Joe put his fork down. 'Why should being a consultant be harder for a woman? The job requires intelligence, not brute strength.'

Dayna's laugh was conciliatory. 'What I meant was they have to be more dedicated. Give up a lot more. Like having a normal marriage or a family.'

'What's a ''normal'' marriage?' Nigel stared across the length of the table at his wife. His tone was almost amused. 'One like ours?'

The undertone of faint sarcasm was unmistakable. Felicity swallowed hurriedly. 'Plenty of female doctors raise families,' she said calmly.

'But it's not the same,' Dayna said with equal

courtesy. 'You have to employ nannies and you don't have much time to spend with the children.'

'You can always make time for what's important.' Felicity's resolve was weakening rapidly. She knew that Joe would register the comment about nannies as a criticism. He would have to employ help when he had Samantha living with him.

Joe's quietly controlled tone confirmed her suspicion. 'Maybe the quality of time with your children is just as important as the quantity is, Dayna.'

'Not for young children,' Dayna responded firmly.

Felicity's resolve fled. 'Perhaps I'll find someone who wants to be a house-husband,' she suggested lightly. 'Then I can keep my job and not worry about who's looking after my children.'

Dayna's smile could only be considered smug. 'I can't imagine many men would find that an attractive prospect. I know Nigel would never have contemplated it.' The look Felicity received held a hint of triumph. 'And I'm sure Joe wouldn't either.' Her face softened as she smiled at Joe. 'Would you, Joe?'

'Oh, I don't know,' Joe said thoughtfully. 'It could have its advantages.'

Felicity slipped her foot out of her shoe and kicked Joe gently under the table as Dayna's face tightened noticeably. This was quite awful enough, without Joe helping to wind his ex-sister-in-law up. Joe's face gave no sign of having received the message.

'Of course, nobody would have me for a house-husband because I can't cook to save myself. Unlike you, Dayna. This really is superb.'

How had Joe managed to get his own shoe off so unobtrusively and rapidly? Felicity had trouble swallowing her mouthful of sautéed courgettes as she felt the toes within his sock slip under the flared hem of her jeans. She reached for her glass of iced water.

'This *is* a lovely meal, Dayna. I must get your recipe for this salad.'

Nigel topped up Felicity's glass of water then glanced briefly at Dayna. 'Speaking of children, where are ours?'

'Andrew's staying the night with a friend and Scott's on the internet.'

'He spends too much time on that computer.'

'He's talking to his friends. They have a loop thing set up. At least he'll be able to keep in touch with them when we go to Australia. Andrew's saying he'd rather stay here and go to boarding school.'

'That's ridiculous.'

'He doesn't want to leave his friends. It's really not the best time to be shifting him.'

'It's promotion,' Nigel reminded his wife. 'He'll

make new friends.' He pushed his plate away. 'You can't think it's a good idea, surely? Scott would be all on his own.'

'No, he wouldn't.'

'Sam's staying here. Now Andrew wants to stay. Do you want to dump Scott in boarding school as well?' Nigel tipped the wine decanter towards his glass. 'Don't you have enough time as it is for the gym and tennis and doing lunches?'

'We'll discuss this later, Nigel. I think it's time for dessert.'

Felicity had avoided looking at anything other than her plate during this exchange. She glanced up to catch Joe's eye as Dayna stood up. He could have warned her of this extra dimension of marital strife in this family. But Joe wasn't looking in her direction. He was busy stifling a huge yawn.

'You look tired, Joe.' Dayna sounded concerned.

'Sorry,' Joe apologised. 'I didn't get much sleep.' He caught Felicity's eye then and held it just long enough to give her a very pleasant tingle at the thought of what had prevented Joe sleeping.

Dayna moved around the table. She leaned over Joe to pick up his plate. One hand rested on his shoulder.

'I've made your favourite for dessert, Joe. Lemon meringue pie.'

The hand stayed on his shoulder just a fraction

too long. The undertone of Dayna's light comment raised instinctive hackles in Felicity. A new and rather horrible suspicion had just presented itself. Dayna didn't want to keep Samantha purely because she loved the child of her sister. There was yet another dimension to this complicated set of relationships. Dayna wanted to keep the bond that she had with Samantha's father.

Dayna wanted Joe.

CHAPTER SEVEN

'THANK God the hospital called when it did. I couldn't have taken much more of that.'

'How is David Carr?' Felicity cradled the phone with her head against her shoulder as she poured her first cup of coffee on Sunday morning. 'Did you find the cause for the increased ischaemia in his fingers?'

'Yes. It just needed a bit of fine tuning. The vascular surgeon got it sorted pretty much by herself. David's actually got some sensation in his thumb and forefinger this morning.'

'That's great.'

'Sure is. He may get some useful mobility back eventually. Sorry I rushed you off like that last night. I didn't really need to be there at all. I just wanted to know what was going on.'

'I understand. You can't put that much effort into a patient without becoming seriously interested in the follow-up.' Felicity sipped her coffee. 'And don't apologise. I wasn't sorry to get away at all. I see what you mean about Dayna. She's not the easiest person to deal with, is she?'

'Never has been. She tried to get between me and Catherine once—before we got married.'

'Why?' Felicity thought she already knew the answer but was Joe aware of how Catherine's sister felt about him?

'I've got no idea,' Joe said. 'It's not as if Catherine was getting something Dayna didn't have. She was married to Nigel by then and had two kids. More than enough to keep her out of mischief, I would have thought.'

Maybe she hadn't had what she'd *really* wanted, Felicity thought. 'She's not a very contented person,' she said aloud.

'No, but that's not my problem,' Joe said wearily. 'And she's certainly not going to use my daughter to try and solve it.'

'What have you got planned for Samantha today? You've got the day off, haven't you?'

'Yes. I just popped into the hospital to see how David was. I'm on my way to collect Sam now. I don't know what we'll do with the rest of the day. Any ideas?'

'Actually, I have.' Felicity smiled into the telephone receiver. 'I had a visitor earlier this morning. Charlie Begg has the farm behind my property and he's always up at dawn.'

'Was there a reason for this visit?' Joe sounded so obviously suspicious that Felicity laughed aloud.

'Charlie's at least seventy years old. I've known him all my life and he's the closest thing to a real relative that I have. It's his son, Graham, who manages the farm these days. Charlie saw the party ponies when they were here and he wanted to know the name of the woman who runs the business. Graham has a friend who's trying to find a home for a little Welsh pony. Quite old and very quiet apparently, and Charlie thought he'd be perfect as a party pony.'

'Sounds ideal.'

'Hmm. I had another idea.' Felicity bit her lip. Would Joe think she was pushing him too quickly here? 'I thought I could take the pony on,' she said cautiously. 'I've got half an acre of orchard here and a stable. It was quite enough for the pony I had as a child.'

'Won't it be too small for you to ride?'

Felicity chuckled. 'I was thinking about Sam. It won't matter if the pony doesn't get ridden very often. It needs a good home to retire to as much as anything, and I'd enjoy having one around again. It would be nice for Sam when she comes to visit. And for my friends' children,' Felicity added casually. There seemed to be a rather thoughtful silence on the other end of the line. 'I thought I might get some hens again as well. They don't take much looking after and a few more animals around the place would be good. It would give Rusty a bit of company when I'm not here.'

'It's a brilliant idea,' Joe told her.

'Anyway, I was going to go and have a look at this pony this afternoon. If you're not doing anything special, maybe you and Sam would like to come along.'

'We'd love to.' Joe sounded delighted. 'And then we'll all go out for dinner. Early dinner. I'll need to get Sam into bed in good time. She's staying with me tonight and there's school in the morning.' An anxious note crept into Joe's tone. 'Can you give me any ideas of what I should put in Sam's lunchbox?'

The pony was twenty-five years old, very fat and very gentle. Samantha fell in love with him instantly.

'What's his name?' Felicity asked.

'Blackie.' The pony's owner looked a little embarrassed. 'Not very original, I know, but my daughter named him when he was born.'

'Sam and I are into naming things according to colour.' Felicity grinned. 'It's a great name, isn't it, Sam?'

'Yep.' Samantha was picking handfuls of grass that Blackie definitely didn't need to eat.

'We're going to hate parting with him but my daughter's been overseas for years now and my wife and I are moving to a flat in town. This place is too much for us now.'

'He'll have a very good home,' Felicity assured the owner. 'And I promise I won't let him go anywhere else in his lifetime.' She watched as Joe showed Samantha how to hold her hand flat to feed the grass to Blackie. They were too engrossed in the experience to be listening.

'He's still got a few good years for being ridden,' Blackie's owner said confidently. 'And he'll be great company for another pony when your daughter's ready for something with a bit more go.'

Her daughter. Felicity didn't bother to correct him. Instead, she made arrangements to have the pony delivered. He arrived on Tuesday evening and Felicity rang Joe on Wednesday morning as soon as she arrived at work.

'Blackie loves the orchard. He looks like he's always lived there. You'll have to come out and see him.'

'How about tonight?'

'Sounds great.' Felicity was hoping it wasn't her that Colin was waiting to speak to. 'I'll cook dinner. Eight o'clock all right for you?'

'Perfect. Don't forget dessert,' Joe said. 'I hear you make great chocolate cake.' His voice deepened. 'I love chocolate icing.'

Felicity allowed the very pleasurable wave of desire just a moment's indulgence. Colin had stepped closer. It *was* her he wished to consult.

'Actually, I don't think I can wait till eight. Are you busy?'

Felicity was nodding at Colin. ''Fraid so. I'd better go.'

'So had I. The anaesthetist is waving at me. I'll come down when we're through here and hope I can catch a quieter spell. I've got something I want to show you.'

Colin looked relieved as Felicity hung up the phone. 'I could use your help,' he said apologetically. 'I've got a case in Resus 2. Twenty-eight-year-old woman—Holly Scott. She's come in with a PV haemorrhage. Looks like a miscarriage but she denies any possibility of pregnancy and refuses to give a urine sample or have an internal examination. There's something going on that I can't put my finger on. I thought that talking to another woman might help. She looks scared to me.'

'Who brought her in?'

'Her husband. Her sister's with her as well.'

'Why don't you take them both to the relatives' room?' Felicity suggested. 'I'll have a quiet chat with Holly and see if I can find out anything.'

Holly Scott looked pale and miserable.

'I'm Fliss Munroe,' Felicity said. 'I'm one of the

consultants here. You're having a pretty serious bleed at present, I gather.'

'It's my period. It's just a bit heavier than usual, that's all. I don't know what all this fuss is about.'

Felicity was reading the ambulance patient report form. 'You fainted at home. Has that ever happened to you before when you have your period?'

'No, but I've probably got a bug or something.'

'Are your periods regular?'

'Always.'

'When was the last one? Can you remember what day it started?'

Holly shook her head. Colin was right, Felicity decided. She looked scared.

'You could be pregnant without necessarily knowing about it, Holly. Sometimes periods continue for a while. The blood tests will tell us soon enough.'

'Oh, God.' Holly buried her face in her hands. 'Can you tell from my blood? I thought pregnancy tests were always done on urine.'

'Just a different test.' Felicity put her hand on Holly's shoulder. 'Do you want to tell me what the problem is, Holly?'

'Barry doesn't have to know, does he? If I'm pregnant?'

'Not unless you choose to tell him. I'm not going

to break patient confidentiality and nor will any of the other staff here.'

'I don't want Georgia to know either.'

'Is that your sister?'

Holly nodded and then burst into tears. 'This is such an awful mess,' she sobbed.

Felicity waited quietly. She handed Holly a box of tissues and the young woman blew her nose and collected herself a minute or so later.

'Barry was overseas for six weeks,' she informed Felicity. 'So he'll know the baby wasn't his. Unless I tell him I was further along than I really was. Could I do that?'

'That's entirely up to you,' Felicity responded. 'How far along do you think you are?'

'About ten weeks.'

'Did you do a pregnancy test yourself?'

Holly nodded miserably. 'Twice. It was positive both times.'

Felicity mirrored the nod. Holly was going to need an internal examination to see if the miscarriage was complete. She might need to be admitted for a dilatation and curettage.

'I couldn't tell anybody. Not even Georgia. Especially not Georgia.'

'Why was that?'

Holly looked agonised. 'Because John is the father of the baby.'

'And John is?'

'Georgia's husband. My brother-in-law.'

Felicity blinked. Holly did have a bit of a mess on her hands.

'Georgie and I have always been close. We still spend a lot of time together. I never meant to fall in love with John. It just happened. I don't know what we're going to do.'

'The first thing to do is sort out the most immediate problem,' Felicity told her. 'It's highly likely that you're having a spontaneous abortion and have either lost or will lose this baby. We're going to need to examine you and maybe do an ultrasound test to see what's going on. You may need surgery as well, but it's a minor operation to clean things up and you'll probably be able to go home later today or tomorrow morning.' She smiled at Holly. 'Nobody has to know anything you don't want them to know, but we can't lie on your behalf. I suggest we tell your family that this is a miscarriage and hope they don't want to enquire too closely about dates.'

'I really wanted this baby,' Holly whispered. 'Maybe it's a punishment.'

Felicity shook her head. 'Of course it's not. About twenty-five per cent of women experience first trimester bleeding. About half of those will end up in miscarriage. It's very common but it doesn't mean it will necessarily happen next time.'

Maybe by the next time Holly would have sorted out the emotional disaster her life was heading towards. Felicity filled Colin in on the background and left him shaking his head over the case as she continued with what turned out to be a busy morning in the emergency department. It was purely fortuitous that Joe chose her belated break as the time to visit the department. He was still in theatre scrubs and he carried a folded newspaper under his arm.

'Wait till you see this,' he told her. 'It's fantastic.'

'Come into my office,' Felicity invited. 'I can make us a coffee there and it's quieter. I could do with a proper break from this place. It's been quite a morning.'

Joe had the newspaper opened on her desk when she handed him the cup of coffee. 'Look at this. They've advertised the consultancy position at Coronation Hospital.'

'The job you've been waiting for?'

'Absolutely.' Joe looked excited. 'I know a lot of neurosurgeons don't want to touch anything outside the skull but I'm still half-orthopaedic. I love anything to do with spinal surgery. And they've got some interesting research programmes going on, using cordotomy and rhizotomy for pain control and neurosurgical management of spastic conditions.

That's something I got interested in while I was in the States.'

'Sounds perfect.' Felicity smiled. 'I'm sure you'll get the job.' She scanned the advertisement. 'This is only a five-tenths position, though. It's not full time.'

'That's because most surgeons want a private practice as well, but it makes it even better for me. I'd have more than enough time to spend with Sam. Maybe I won't need a live-in nanny. Dayna's been warning me about how horrendously expensive that would be.'

'Is that going to be a problem?' Felicity was surprised. Joe should be fairly comfortable financially by his age. Even if he'd lost income doing his postgraduate training he'd had years of employment as a consultant surgeon before then.

'I'll manage on five-tenths. I might not be able to afford to take on a mortgage for a while but having Sam with me is far more important. I'm sure I can find a real house for us to rent.'

Felicity frowned. 'Look, tell me if it's none of my business, Joe, but I'm surprised you can't afford a house. Was the training in the States that expensive?'

'That was only part of it,' Joe told her. 'The trips home to see Sam were costly and I paid for Dayna and the boys to bring her over for a trip to

Disneyland last year. I've covered all Sam's expenses while she's been with Dayna and then I helped my parents buy their unit in the retirement village.' He gave the lopsided smile that went straight to Felicity's heart. 'Sorry, love, but at least everybody will know you're not after me for my money.'

Felicity laughed. 'Maybe you're after me for mine.'

'Hardly. I'm after you for your chocolate icing.' Joe leaned forward and placed a soft kiss on Felicity's lips. Then he drew her into his arms and kissed her neck. Felicity hugged him back. She wasn't bothered by Joe's lack of financial security. She had more than enough money for both of them and the evidence of Joe's generosity was touching. What bothered her was the thought of him sending money home for Samantha's expenses and paying for her foster-family to have a holiday that must have cost a small fortune. One look at the Jacksons' house would be enough to convince anybody that they had no need of any of Joe's money. Why had Dayna allowed Joe to do that?

'So, why did you need the escape from your morning?' Joe released Felicity and picked up his coffee. 'Has it been bad?'

'Not really. Just busy.'

Joe's cellphone rang just as Felicity was about to

start telling him of her first case of the day. Joe unclipped the phone from his belt, frowning when he saw the caller display. He cut off the ringing.

'Voice mail will do for that call,' he told Felicity wryly. 'Dayna finds something to call me about at least once every day. It's easier to collect the messages and deal with them all at once when I ring Sam in the evening.'

Felicity was still thinking about her first case and the complicated problems Holly Scott had to deal with. The reminder of Dayna and further evidence of her bond with Joe was more than a little disturbing.

'Tell me something, Joe,' Felicity tried to keep her tone casual. 'Were Dayna and Catherine close sisters?'

'Very close.' Joe didn't seem bothered by the sudden change in conversational direction.

'They must have spent a lot of time together.'

'We were all living in Wellington when Catherine and I got married. They did see a lot of each other.'

'Were Dayna and Nigel happy together then?'

'They seemed to be.' Joe frowned. 'But maybe not. Nigel travelled a lot in those days. Dayna relied on Catherine's company.' Joe noticed the odd expression on Felicity's face. 'Why do you ask?'

'I had a case to deal with this morning. Spontaneous abortion. The woman had become pregnant to her brother-in-law so she was terrified of her husband or sister finding out.'

'That's understandable.' Joe was staring at Felicity. 'Good grief, Fliss—you don't think there was ever anything going on between me and Dayna, do you?'

'Of course not.' Felicity's response was swift. Joe's astonishment was palpably sincere and she wasn't going to admit her nasty suspicions. Maybe the interest was purely on Dayna's side. Or maybe she had just imagined it.

'The only thing going on between me and Dayna is rather a lot of arguing,' Joe continued. 'We started a great one on Monday night when I took Sam home. They've got tickets booked for Australia. They're going for a week to go house-hunting.'

'Is Sam going as well?'

'No,' Joe said very firmly. 'This time I've put my foot down. She's staying with me for the week.'

'Good.'

'Dayna doesn't think so. She said Sam can't sleep on a couch for a week. I said I'd sleep on the couch. Sam is welcome to my bed. Then she wanted to know what I was going to do about my working hours.'

So far, it didn't seem entirely unreasonable. 'What *are* you going to do?' Felicity could see that it wouldn't be easy unless Joe planned to get some kind of leave.

'My days off are Monday and Tuesday. I'm going to ring a nanny agency and find some daytime help for the rest of the week and my parents have offered to help. Sam can stay with them on the night I'm on call.'

'That's kind of them. How are your parents?'

Joe gave her a speculative look. 'OK, I know they're not fighting fit but they're not nearly as decrepit as Dayna likes to make out. They're quite capable of caring for their granddaughter for short periods of time.'

'I'm not suggesting otherwise. I just wondered how they were.'

Joe sighed. 'Dad's very limited by his respiratory problems and Mum's diabetes is getting harder to control. I think she's going to lose her eyesight completely and she's been getting short of breath lately. She's had a few niggly chest pains as well. I've got her booked in for a cardiology check-up but that's not for a few weeks yet.'

Felicity had to admit that asking too much of Joe's parents wouldn't be a good idea. 'When did you say your days off were?'

'Monday and Tuesday.'

Felicity glanced up at the roster on her pinboard. 'Mine are Wednesday and Thursday. I could help.'

'Would you?' A hopeful light gleamed in Joe's dark eyes. 'That would be so great, Fliss.' He grinned cheekily. 'I was kind of hoping you'd say that.'

Felicity stared at Joe thoughtfully. She ignored the sound of her pager for a second. She also ignored the emotional warning bell that tried to sound. Had Joe been *hoping* she'd offer to help with child care or had he *expected* it? Was her ability to act as a surrogate mother an attractive advantage that she possessed? As attractive as her secure financial position and the property she owned, perhaps? The thought was fleeting and easily dismissed. She'd made assumptions about Joe's marital status and personality when she'd first met him that had been entirely unfounded and could have been very destructive. She wasn't about to make that mistake again.

'We could do this together, Joe. Why don't you and Sam come and stay with me for the week? The first four days aren't going to be a problem and we can juggle the other days. What time do you start work on Friday?'

'Seven a.m.'

'I don't start till nine. I could drop Sam at school on my way to work.'

'I don't finish until five, though. I guess my parents could collect Sam.'

'Let's try and do this all by ourselves.' Felicity

really wanted to do this. It would give Joe the confidence that he could manage and then Dayna would have no hope of stalling the change of Samantha's living arrangements any longer. 'Lots of schools these days have an after-school care programme. Does Sam's?'

'I don't know. I'll check.'

'The weekend shouldn't be a problem. Charlie's granddaughter is seventeen. She'd probably be delighted to have some babysitting employment.'

'Would she?' Joe was looking positively excited now.

'I'll check.' Felicity's pager sounded again. 'I think my break's over. I'll see you tonight, Joe, and we'll finalise our plans.'

Joe kissed her briefly but firmly. 'You're amazing,' he said, and promptly kissed her again. 'And I love you. Sam will be so excited by this plan of yours.'

'It'll be fun,' Felicity responded. 'For all of us.'

'Fun' wasn't nearly the right adjective to describe the following week.

It was magic.

How could Felicity have ever looked forward to returning home after work before? How could she not have realised how lonely her existence had been?

To have a small girl running excitedly to greet her as she stepped out of her car, bursting to relay the enthralling events of the day at school and what she had done with virtually every moment since, was a totally novel experience.

To have a man waiting to greet her with a face that advertised joy in her presence and arms that conveyed a security that that joy was not about to fade was the most wonderful feeling in the world.

Joe's cooking wasn't anywhere near as bad as he'd made out. On Monday he made a pasta dish, admittedly with a store-bought sauce, but on Tuesday he grilled steaks and made a creditable version of Dayna's warm vegetable salad. He shrugged off Felicity's praise though he was clearly rather pleased with himself.

'I've watched Dayna do it a few times over the years. It's one of her stand-bys.'

Even better were the two days that Felicity had off when Joe was at work. She had plenty of time to herself and actually enjoyed the extra housework her guests necessitated. After school on Wednesday Felicity and Samantha saddled up Blackie and Felicity led the pony for a walk down the road with Rusty following closely behind. The spring weather was glorious and Felicity wasn't surprised to meet Charlie taking his Jack Russell terrier for a walk.

'How's the pony working out?'

'He's lovely.' Blackie nudged Felicity's armpit as she stopped. She rubbed the velvety nose.

'I can ride now,' Samantha informed Charlie.

'I can see that.' Charlie slipped Felicity the ghost of a wink. Samantha's small legs were sticking out at an odd angle because of the rotund shape of Blackie's stomach. Her hands were fisted through the fluffy black mane.

Felicity grinned. 'I'd forgotten how nice it was to have animals in the garden. I think I might bring the hen-house out of retirement. Fresh eggs taste so much better. You don't know anyone with some spare hens by any chance, do you, Charlie?'

'Bound to.' Charlie nodded. 'Leave it with me.'

The crate of hens arrived on Thursday afternoon, along with a bale of hay to line nesting boxes and a sack of grain for feed.

'You're a wonderful neighbour, Charlie. Thank you.'

'I talked to Sarah-Jane about the babysitting you mentioned over the weekend. She's happy to do it. Just let her know what times you need her.'

A minor hiccup occurred with arrangements on Saturday. Felicity was rostered to work from eight a.m. to four p.m. Joe had a ward round to do, starting at eight-thirty a.m. and Sarah Jane had swimming training she couldn't miss that wouldn't finish until nine.

'I'll just have to be late for my ward round, I guess.' Joe sounded resigned. 'And hope that it's not reflected in the references I get for my next job.'

'Let me see if I can juggle my roster,' Felicity offered. 'Whoever's on for the night might be happy to stay a bit longer, and I can return the favour another day.'

Felicity was proud of the ease with which she made the arrangement that ironed out the minor complication. The appreciation Joe displayed made it more than worthwhile.

'Fliss?' His tone was serious. 'You're fantastic. I'm beginning to wonder what I would do without you in my life.' He held out his arms. 'Come here.'

Felicity was reminded of the pleasure gained from Joe's appreciation when she arrived late to start her shift on Saturday. She was also beginning to wonder what she would do without Joe in *her* life and the concern deepened considerably after she arrived home that afternoon to find Joe hard at work in her garden, pruning back perennials and digging out weeds. She stood and watched for a moment from the other side of the lawn. Joe took one look at her face when she joined him and put down his spade.

'Bad day?'

Felicity nodded. Joe pulled off his gardening gloves and hugged her. Then he turned her body so that she was facing one of the garden benches.

'Come on,' he instructed. 'Sit down and tell me all about it.'

So she did. She told him about the ethical dilemma she had faced with a case that afternoon and how she was unable to decide whether she had, in fact, done the right thing. The patient had been a man in his early forties with terminal cancer. He had suffered a cardiac arrest at home and his wife—a nurse—had been there to administer cardio-pulmonary resuscitation. The man had begged Felicity to document a non-resuscitation order if he arrested again. He'd had enough. His wife had begged her to do everything she could to keep him alive. She couldn't bear to be without him, and the children just needed a little more time with their father.

'What did you do?'

'I spent half the day hoping that nothing would happen while he was under my care. We arranged transfer to a hospice with the thought that better symptom control might make the time he had left more bearable.' Felicity stared at her hands. 'I spent the rest of the day thinking about how ghastly it had been, breaking the news to his wife and children that he'd died.'

'Did you try and resuscitate him?'

Felicity was silent for a long minute. 'No,' she said finally. 'We had already decided to honour his request. He knew exactly what he wanted and how badly he wanted it. He'd hung on as long as he could for the sake of his family but, Joe, you should have seen his wife's face. And he had a little girl about Samantha's age. I told her how sorry I was and how I wished I could have done more. And I meant every word. I regretted not having tried. I thought maybe I'd made the wrong decision.'

'No.' Joe shook his head gently. 'He was going to die, Felicity. Even if he'd lived a few more hours or days or even weeks it wouldn't have made it any easier for his family. It may very well not have been a successful resuscitation if you had tried, and if it had been he certainly wouldn't have thanked you. You gave him something important, Fliss. The dignity of autonomous choice and the respect that his wishes mattered. You did the right thing. Exactly the same thing I would have done.'

He drew Felicity into his arms and her deep sigh was largely one of relief. It wasn't the first haunting case she had managed. It wouldn't be the last. The acceptance of her actions didn't require the usual endless hours of introspection this time, however. The opportunity to share the experience and receive understanding reassurance was enough to allow Felicity a new perspective in separating her home and professional lives. The distraction provided by Samantha as she ran across the lawn towards them, with Rusty trotting faithfully beside her, added a fitting punctuation mark. The door could be shut on professional matters for the moment. The understanding of what their work could entail was there on both sides and there was more to life than work. A lot more.

'It's an *egg*!' Samantha shouted as soon as she came close enough. 'Fliss! Daddy! *Look!* It's a real egg.'

The hens provided more eggs on Sunday but not quickly enough for Samantha. Ten trips to the henhouse yielded only three still very warm eggs.

'Is there a chicken inside them, Fliss?'

'No. There won't be a chick inside them unless we get a rooster.'

'Why?'

Felicity looked towards Joe for assistance. He grinned and remained annoyingly silent.

'The hens are mothers,' Felicity told Samantha. 'Chicks need a father as well. That's the rooster.'

'I've got a father,' Samantha stated. 'But I haven't got a real mother. She's dead.'

'I know.' Felicity tried to match her tone to Samantha's clear statement of fact. 'That's sad, isn't it?'

'Mmm.' Samantha had only been temporarily distracted. 'Can we get a rooster, Fliss? Please? I think the hens are lonely.'

'Why not?' Felicity smiled. 'We don't want lonely hens.'

Joe waited until they were alone, sitting at the kitchen table over coffee after Samantha had gone to bed, to shake his head sadly at Felicity.

'As an opportunity to advance my daughter's sex education that was a dismal failure, Felicity Munroe. And here I was relying on you to fulfil that particular gap for me.'

'It was all she wanted or needed to know right now,' Felicity said. 'If she'd wanted to know more she would have asked.'

'Maybe the opportunity will arise again if you get a rooster and we start having chicks running around. Are you really going to get one, Fliss? Do you want to get woken at the crack of dawn every day?'

'I don't mind,' Felicity assured him. She grinned. 'I don't want the hens being lonely.'

'I don't want to be lonely either,' Joe said slowly. 'I think that I might get unbearably lonely if I was away from you for any length of time, Fliss.'

'Do you?' Felicity knew exactly how Joe felt. She felt the same way.

'Dayna rang while you were at work today.' Disappointingly, Joe seemed to be changing the subject.

'Dayna has rung every day.' Felicity sighed. She was beginning to feel like not answering the telephone in her own house. When she did it was patently obvious that Joe was the only person Dayna wished to converse with. She didn't approve of Felicity aiding and abetting Joe over the arrangements for this week. Maybe she knew she was now outnumbered.

'This time was different,' Joe said. 'No questions about things that could have possibly gone wrong and no complaints. She sounded happy. They've found the perfect house and she wanted to tell Sam how wonderful it is. It even has a nearby paddock with horses in it. Then she told me it has a granny flat. She suggested that it could be the perfect solution for all of us.'

'Could it?' Felicity searched Joe's expression looking for reassurance that he didn't agree with Dayna. She found it.

'Of course not,' he added for good measure. 'Samantha doesn't even want to go back to Cashmere with the Jacksons. She wants to stay here—with us.'

'I love having her here. The house really feels alive again.'

'I want to stay here, too—with us,' Joe said softly. 'This week has been just perfect, Fliss.'

Felicity nodded her agreement. 'We've been like a real family, haven't we?'

'And it's run like clockwork, despite our jobs and awkward rosters. We managed.'

'We did.'

'We could do it, you know, Fliss. We could have it all. Our careers, each other and a real family. We could have a child of our own—a brother or sister for Sam.'

Felicity's gaze was glued to Joe's face. He was right. The week *had* been perfect. Almost perfect. Now Joe had presented an even more enticing scenario—one for the future. They *could* have it all. Felicity wanted to have it all. She had never wanted anything this much in her life.

'I love you so much, Fliss. I want to marry you. I want to have you with me every day for the rest of my life.'

'I feel the same way, Joe. I love you *and* Sam.'

'Does that make the decision harder for you? Having Sam as part of the deal, I mean.'

'I've never made an easier decision, Joe. Some things are too right to argue about, and marrying you is one of those things.' Felicity paused, a tiny smile hovering. 'So, if you get around to actually asking me to marry you I might very well say yes.'

Joe held her gaze. 'Felicity Munroe, I love you. Will you marry me?'

Felicity matched his serious tone. 'Yes. Of course I will.' Her smile couldn't escape before Joe's lips claimed her but she managed a few more words. 'I thought you'd never ask.'

CHAPTER EIGHT

THE engagement ring was quite beautiful.

It came from a very unexpected source. Joe wanted his parents to be the first to know their news. They hadn't told Samantha, having decided that it would be unfair to expect a five-year-old child to keep a secret like that.

'As soon as Dayna hears she'll know that her time with Sam is almost over. I need to find the right time to tell her myself.'

'Do you want me to be there as well?'

'No. Best I have a quiet talk to her alone, I think.'

Felicity nodded her understanding. Dayna could well be prompted to reminisce about the last wedding Joe had planned—with her sister, Catherine. Maybe they both had a few ghosts to lay to rest.

Joe's parents were thrilled with the news. They toasted the couple with sherry when Joe took Felicity to visit them in their retirement village unit later that week. Felicity swallowed the sweet sherry and tried not to grimace. Distraction seemed a good idea.

'This is a lovely place.' She gazed around the tiny unit. There was just one bedroom with an *en suite* bathroom fitted to cope with any disabilities an elderly couple might have. The kitchen was equally practical and the sitting room just large enough to handle a few visitors comfortably. Treasured items of furniture, ornaments and pictures filled all the spaces, but the effect was homely rather than cluttered.

'It's just right for us.' Donald Petersen nodded. 'And Norma loves it. There's a keen bowling team in the village and weekly bus trips somewhere interesting if we fancy an outing.'

'We went all the way to Akaroa last week,' Norma told Felicity. 'We had lunch and looked in the art galleries. It was a lovely day.' Norma put down her sherry glass and smiled at Felicity. 'I'm just so happy about you and Joe. I wonder...'

'Wonder what, Mum?' Joe prompted.

'I was just thinking. You haven't bought an engagement ring yet, have you?'

'No.' Joe smiled at Felicity. 'We will, very soon.'

'I can't wear mine any more. My finger's got fat.' Norma was a little hesitant. 'It's not just the offer of a hand-me-down ring, love. This one's rather special. It was worn by my grandmother and she gave it to me when I got engaged to Don. The band has been remade but the ring's still basically original. Would you like to see it?'

'I'd love to,' Felicity responded.

The antique ring was an intricate knot of white gold and tiny diamonds that gave the impression of a tiny garland of flowers.

'Try it on,' Norma urged. 'See if it fits.'

It did fit. Perfectly. Felicity loved it. Joe loved the idea of her wearing his great-grandmother's ring. Norma and Donald were honoured to provide such a symbolic gift.

Gareth was stunned, both by the ring and the news that came when he noticed Felicity wearing the ring a few days later.

'I knew it. I could feel there was something going on right from that first time Joe was in this department. The day you insisted on looking after his daughter's broken arm.'

'There wasn't anything going on then,' Felicity demurred.

'Ha!' Gareth winked at Joe. 'And then you were pumping me for information about whether Fliss had a significant other in her life.'

'I never did,' Joe protested. 'You brought up that topic of conversation all by yourself.'

'Only because I knew you wanted to find out.' Gareth moved on with a benevolent smile. 'I love working in Emergency,' he was heard to murmur. 'Always something interesting going on.'

Joe and Felicity exchanged a smile. 'So, what interesting thing did you summon me for, Fliss?'

'Two things. One, how did your interview at Coronation Hospital go this morning?'

'Couldn't have been better. They're desperate to fill the position and I think they want me.'

'Of course they do and not just because they're desperate.'

'They've got permission to have a locum fill the position until they appoint someone permanent.' Joe grinned triumphantly. 'I'm starting there in two weeks' time.'

'Really? That's fantastic Joe.'

'Isn't it just? I've handed my resignation in here already.'

'Well, just before you pack your bags, could you look at these X-rays for me?' Felicity led the way to the viewing screens. 'This is a sixty-five-year-old man who came in with sudden-onset, low back pain that gets worse when he lies down. Sharp ten out of ten pain that radiates to his leg. He has weakness and pins and needles in both legs and tenderness over his lower back at L3, L4 level.'

'Any rab results back yet?'

Joe went over the available laboratory test results before turning his attention to the X-ray screen. His opinion was that the spinal problems were being caused by secondary bone involvement from a malignancy elsewhere in the body.

'The chest X-ray was clear and Colin didn't find anything obvious on physical examination. I might check him over myself.'

'I'd guess a breast or prostate malignancy.'

Felicity sighed. 'Not a great outlook if the primary lesion has already metastasised to this extent.'

'No. We can use surgery for decompression and relieve some of the symptoms but it will only be buying a bit of time. He'll need radiation therapy and high-dose steroids. I'd get Oncology down to see him first. They can call us in when he's ready for surgery.'

'Thanks, Joe.' Felicity pulled the X-rays down. 'I knew we were dealing with something nasty when Colin asked me to look at these. I'm going to miss having you available for quick consults like this.'

'I'll be available for you any time.' Joe was smiling as Colin approached them. 'Just call me.'

'I'd better go over these with Colin.' Felicity switched on the viewing screen again and slipped the X-rays back into position. 'Will I see you tonight?'

'I'm on call tonight.'

'Tomorrow, then? It'll have to be late, I'm afraid. I don't finish till eleven.'

'I'll be looking forward to it,' Joe said.

'Hey! Congratulations. I heard the news.' Colin shook Joe's hand. 'You're a lucky man.'

'So are you.' Joe grinned. 'Fliss is going to test you on your X-ray interpretation skills.' He paused as he turned away. Felicity caught the signal and walked with him for a step or two.

'I told Dayna, by the way. Last night.'

'Oh.' Felicity bit her lip. 'What did she say?'

'Not much. She rang me this morning, though. She's agreed to let us tell Sam by ourselves and she wants us to go for a celebratory drink. First clear night for us both seems to be next Wednesday. Shall I pencil it in?'

'Sure.' The weekend would present a good opportunity to tell Samantha about the upcoming changes in her life. So far, Dayna's reaction seemed positive so maybe there wouldn't be any unpleasant repercussions from Samantha talking about it later. The visit on Wednesday would let them know what the atmosphere was like for Samantha, and if it was difficult in any way Felicity planned to ask Joe and his daughter to move in with her permanently. There was really no need to wait for a wedding.

Samantha accepted the news as though she hadn't expected anything else. 'So this will be my house, too?'

'It will indeed.' Joe stood back after his cuddle and let Felicity answer the questions.

'And Rusty will be my dog?'

'He thinks he is already.'

'And the hens? And Blackie?'

'They'll all be part of our family. You and Daddy and me and all the animals.'

'So if you marry Daddy, will I still call you Fliss or can I call you Mummy?'

Felicity swallowed the unexpected lump in her throat. 'You can call me whatever you like, sweetheart.'

'I think I'll call you Mummy. I'd like that.'

'So would I.' Felicity kissed the child. 'Goodnight, pet.'

'You handled that brilliantly,' Joe told her as they headed downstairs together.

'It wasn't difficult.' Felicity responded. 'Let's just hope that any questions Dayna has are as easy to answer.'

Felicity wasn't going to feel underdressed on this visit to the Jackson household. She wore a simple, close-fitting, sleeveless black dress. She tamed her long hair into a French braid that was even less casual than her usual work style of a ponytail or knot. Make-up was attended to carefully and Felicity added a string of pearls that had belonged to her grandmother as a final touch.

Joe whistled silently in admiration when he arrived to collect her. 'You look stunning, Fliss. I should go home and change.' Joe was wearing faded jeans and a casual, short-sleeved, open-necked cream shirt.

'You look fine. I just thought I should make a bit of an effort. I didn't feel appropriately dressed last time and it didn't make things any more comfortable.'

'I think tonight will be a lot better,' Joe commented during their drive. 'Dayna seems to have accepted things now. She's been quite different ever since she heard about our engagement.'

'Really?' Felicity was wary. 'In what way?'

'She was pretty quiet for a few days. Thinking things over, I guess. She seems to have turned over a new leaf since. I think she's pleased. About us and about my job.'

'That's great.' The faintly dubious tone was impossible to hide.

Joe parked the car and switched off the ignition, glancing at Felicity after a short pause. 'Dayna's bound to have some mixed feelings,' he said carefully. 'She's losing what she considers to be a daughter and I'm finding a replacement for her sister in my life.'

'Is that what I am, Joe?' The thought was disturbing.

'Only as far as Dayna is concerned.' Joe touched

Felicity's cheek with a soft stroke of his thumb. 'I did love Catherine and I held onto the memories of the best times we had together, but now I have you and those memories could never be enough.'

'Do you think about her a lot?'

'Not nearly as often as I used to and almost never when I'm with you. I love you, Fliss. I want to spend my life with you and make the most of every moment we have together. There will always be reminders of Catherine—she gave birth to Sam, after all—but those reminders can't affect what we have. I know it's not going to be easy for you and Dayna but she's been a mother to Sam since she was born. I can't cut her out of our lives completely.'

'I wouldn't expect you to.'

'Just don't let her upset you by anything she might say. Try and see things from her point of view. I know you have the generosity of spirit to do that.'

'I will. Don't worry, Joe.'

'You might even be surprised. Maybe Dayna has accepted things enough to be genuinely happy for us.'

Dayna did seem genuinely happy. And accommodating. Had she dressed casually because she knew Felicity had felt uncomfortable on her last visit? Not that her designer jeans and close fitting T-shirt could be considered in any way scruffy. The glass of Scotch in Dayna's hand was almost empty. The smile on her face was bright.

'I thought we'd just have a family barbecue tonight. The weather's so nice and the children will enjoy it. They're having a swim at the moment. Nigel, darling, find Joe and Felicity a drink. We've got some celebrating to do.'

'We sure have.' Nigel had a tray of flutes and a cold bottle of champagne ready inside. He handed a glass to Felicity first.

'Congratulations,' he said warmly. 'I was absolutely delighted to hear about you and Joe. Couldn't be better news and your timing is perfect. Sam's so excited about the prospect of coming to live with you that I don't think she'll be upset at all when we take off across the ditch.'

Felicity looked past Nigel's shoulder, through the French doors opening to the pool area. Samantha was in a large plastic ring shaped like a duck, being whirled around by Scott. She was shrieking with laughter.

'She certainly looks happy at the moment.'

'Doesn't she?' Dayna helped herself to a glass from the tray. 'Thank heavens for the new heating system otherwise we would have had to wait another month before using the pool. Shame to waste such lovely spring weather. Now, let me see your ring,' she instructed Felicity. 'Mmm. It's quite unusual, isn't it?'

'It's about a hundred years old,' Felicity said. 'It belonged to Joe's great-grandmother.'

'Really?' Dayna glanced at Joe as he accepted a glass of champagne from Nigel. 'Catherine had a brand-new ring. I've kept it for Samantha but I'll wait till she's older to give it to her.'

'I'm sure she'll treasure it,' Felicity said easily. 'She might even want to use it herself one day.'

'Congratulations, Joe,' Nigel was saying. 'It's about time something this good happened for you. You're a lucky man.'

'I am, indeed.'

Nigel raised his glass. 'I'd like to propose a toast here. To Joe and Felicity.'

'When will you hear about the job, Joe?' Dayna didn't let the moment linger.

'Officially the position will be advertised overseas, with applications closing in a month. Unofficially, I've got the job and they've taken me on as a locum until the process is formalised. I start there next week.'

'Is it what you really want, Joe? Are you sure we can't tempt you over to Australia?'

'It's exactly what I want.' Joe sounded confident. 'And it couldn't be in a better place. Coronation Hospital is only two minutes' drive away from

Fliss's house. I'll be able to walk, apart from the theatre sessions I'll still have in Queen Mary's.'

'So you're not planning to move, then?' Dayna asked Felicity. 'You don't want a place that you chose together?'

'We'd never find a better spot,' Joe said quickly. 'And I'd never try and move Felicity from her family home—unless, of course, she wanted to.'

'I don't want to,' Felicity said. 'I don't think I'll ever want to live anywhere else.'

'Then neither will I,' Joe stated. 'Home is where the heart is after all, and Felicity has mine—hook, line and sinker.'

'Hear, hear!' Nigel responded.

Dayna had finished her champagne but declined a refill. 'I'll stick to the Scotch,' she told Nigel. 'Don't worry, I'll do it myself. Why don't you men go and fire up the barbecue?'

'OK.' Nigel was watching the children as he headed outside. 'You'd better slow down, Scott. You'll be making Sam feel sick. Where's Andrew?'

'In the shower.'

'About time you two got dry as well. We'll be cooking dinner soon and we don't want you standing around wet and getting cold.'

Joe and Nigel uncovered the gas barbecue and started the burners. They selected cooking utensils and arranged the meat before opening cans of beer

and getting down to the serious business of super-
vising the cooking. Felicity went to help Dayna in
the kitchen with the salads. She was followed in by
Samantha who was wrapped in a large towel.

'Fliss? Did you see me swim?'

'I did, sweetheart. Did you get dizzy, going round
and round like that?'

'No, it was fun.'

'Samantha loves swimming,' Dayna observed.
She flicked Felicity a glance. 'Have you got a pool?'

'No.' Felicity smiled at Samantha, avoiding further eye contact with Dayna. 'Maybe one day.'

'Go and have a shower now, Samantha,' Dayna
instructed. 'You're dripping all over the floor.'

'Can I have a sausage for my dinner, Mum?'

'Of course.' Dayna smiled but then raised her
eyebrows at Samantha's expression. 'What's the
matter, dear?'

'When Fliss marries Daddy she's going to be my
mummy.'

'She'll be your stepmother.' The pitch of Dayna's
voice rose noticeably.

Samantha wasn't going to be distracted by semantics. She was looking worried. 'So if she's my
mummy I won't be able to call you "Mum".'

'Of course you can.' Felicity broke in to try and
defuse the potentially sticky conversation.

'If you want to,' Dayna added tightly.

Samantha looked at each of the women in turn. Felicity recognised the earnest desire to say the right thing and the confusion generated by undercurrents the child had no hope of comprehending. Samantha chose the safest option of remaining silent. Dayna turned away.

'Shower time, Samantha.'

As soon as the child had left the kitchen Dayna rounded on Felicity.

'He doesn't love you, you know. Not really. Not the way he loved Catherine. Or me.'

'Sorry?' Felicity dropped the lettuce leaf, unbroken, into the bowl.

'Think about it, Felicity.' Dayna took another large swallow of her drink. 'Joe came back to New Zealand to be with his daughter. He needed a job and a place to live and one more thing before he could achieve what he wanted.'

'And that was?' Felicity retrieved the lettuce leaf. She pulled it into tiny pieces. She might as well let Dayna have her say.

'Well, we both know how important Joe's career is to him. It was what he used to give himself a reason to live after Catherine died. He's not about to give it up to be a full-time parent. He had to find help for child-care.'

'If that was what Joe wanted he would have gone to an agency. You don't know what you're talking

about, Dayna.' Felicity's intention to try and see
things from Dayna's point of view had already evap-
orated. 'And I have absolutely no interest in listening to you.'

'*Don't* you?' Dayna snarled. 'Try putting two and
two together, Felicity. Joe needed a job. He got one.
He needed a house and he can't afford one at the
moment, but you've got a very nice one and it's
even handy to the new job. All that it will cost is a
year or two of marriage. He needs a nanny. I'll bet
he's suggested you have a baby of your own. He'll
expect you to want to stay home and look after it
and it won't be any extra trouble to look after
Samantha, will it? Much easier and cheaper than trying to hire a nanny. And then there's the extras…
I'll bet he's—'

Felicity walked out as Dayna was still speaking.
She should have walked out much sooner. The best
she could hope for was to be able to ignore this
vicious attack and dismiss it as the nonsense she
knew it was. This seemed a possibility when Dayna
announced she had a migraine and needed to go and
lie down. It seemed more certain when the children
rejoined the adults and Samantha sat on her father's
knee, beaming frequent smiles in Felicity's direction.

The poison laid by Dayna's words seeped in
nonetheless. How did Felicity know that it was *her*

that Joe really wanted and not just an ideal solution to all the issues in his life? Could it be so calculated on Joe's part? There was no question that by marrying her Joe would get a house to live in. A home, no less, complete with pets and the perfect garden for a child to play in. A home close to his exciting new job and close to his child's school. Joe had said to Nigel that he would never try moving her from her family home. That home was where the heart was. Maybe there was some truth in the notion that Joe's heart was where the home was. And he would get a partner who would share the raising of his child. Someone who loved the child, in fact. Felicity had made that quite clear. And he *had* suggested she have a baby of her own.

The alarm bells she'd suppressed that day when Joe had been so pleased with her offer of assistance rang again. And this time Felicity was in no mood to ignore them. Perhaps he had been expecting her to step in as surrogate mother when the Jacksons made their visit to Australia. Maybe it had been a kind of test to see how well she lived up to those expectations. And she'd passed with flying colours, hadn't she? When the hiccup had occurred with Samantha's care on the Saturday morning she'd sorted things out with admirable swiftness by changing her own schedule. Joe hadn't exactly tried to find any other options, had he? Like an alternative baby-sitter, maybe.

No. He'd merely told her she was fantastic and that he wondered what he would do without her in his life. And Felicity had lapped it up. How long had she known Joe? A little over three months? A ridiculously short period of time in which to start trusting someone so completely. Dayna had known him a lot longer than that, and what she had suggested was suddenly making sense. A lot of sense. Of course Joe was wondering what he would do without her in his life. If she disappeared then the perfect little plan for his future would disappear along with her.

She was being used.

No matter how strongly she felt about Joe, she had more self-respect than to allow that to continue.

Joe could sense that the atmosphere wasn't what it should have been. Dayna had clearly had far too much to drink and had gone to sleep it off, but why had Felicity become so quiet? Had Dayna said something when the women had been alone in the kitchen? Joe became increasingly concerned when he noticed how little Felicity was eating. Taking Samantha inside to put her to bed gave him an opportunity to try and find out what was going on. He finished reading a story to his daughter and kissed her goodnight.

'We'll come and get you after school on Friday, Sam.' Joe had the weekend off before starting his new job. 'We'll stay with Fliss for the weekend. You can ride Blackie and feed the hens.'

'Will there be any eggs?'

'Bound to be. Probably lots.'

'Is the rooster there yet?'

'I'm not sure. I'll send Fliss up to say goodnight and you can ask her.'

Joe left Samantha's room. The master bedroom was just along the hallway near the stairs. He knocked briefly on the open door.

'Dayna? Are you feeling any better?'

'I'm fine. Come in, Joe.'

'No. I'm going to take Fliss home.' Joe cleared his throat. 'I just wanted to know if you'd said anything that might have upset her.'

Dayna appeared at the door. She'd taken off her jeans and T-shirt and was wearing a very loosely tied silk robe over her underwear. She stood close enough to prompt Joe to take a step backwards into the hall.

'I didn't say anything that wasn't true, Joe. I know why you want to marry her.'

Joe's hackles rose. 'And why is that?'

'Because you can't have me.' Dayna swayed

slightly as she took another step towards Joe. 'But I've been thinking about that, Joe. I'm ready to leave Nigel. I don't love him any more. Not the way I love you.'

'For God's sake, Dayna.' Joe put his hands up to push Dayna away. 'Stop this. Right now.'

'I can't. And I know you don't want me to.'

The arms around Joe's neck were so tight they were strangling him. He had to use both hands to pry the grip free so there was nothing he could do to prevent Dayna leaning forward to press her mouth against his. Pressing her whole body against his. The force of her new move was enough to take him off balance. He had to let go of Dayna's arms and catch her waist to prevent them both falling. He pushed her away with determination. Dayna staggered back until she made contact with the wall.

'Don't move,' Joe ordered harshly. 'And don't say anything else. I'm going to pack a bag for my daughter and I'm taking her away with me tonight. She is not going to stay in this house for a minute longer than I can possibly help.'

It took a few minutes. Samantha was excited by the change of sleeping arrangements. 'Can Rusty sleep with me tonight?'

'Of course he can. Come on, we'll go and find Fliss and go home.'

But Felicity wasn't to be found downstairs. Nigel was cleaning the barbecue.

'Fliss? She's gone.' Nigel looked puzzled. 'She said she had had an urgent call from the hospital on her cellphone and she took a taxi.' Nigel frowned. 'She said you knew about it. She saw you upstairs.'

Had she? Joe's blood felt as though it had turned to ice. Had she seen Dayna trying to kiss him? And what had Dayna said to her in the kitchen? Dayna's version of the real reason he wanted to marry Felicity was as potentially destructive as it was untrue.

'Why aren't you in bed, Sam?' Nigel was looking concerned even before he noticed the overnight bag. 'Is something going on here that I should know about?'

'Sam's coming home with me,' Joe told him. 'Where she should be. Where she should have been all along.' He scooped Samantha up into his arms and picked up the bag with one hand. 'Sam and I are leaving, Nigel. We won't be coming back.'

'Why not? What's happened?' Nigel followed them towards the car.

'Talk to your wife, Nigel,' Joe advised.

'What's Dayna done?' Nigel demanded. 'Hell, I knew she'd had too much to drink tonight. She's said something, hasn't she? Something that's upset Fliss.'

'You could say that,' Joe agreed grimly.

'She's not a happy woman,' Nigel said quietly. 'And I know it's partly my fault. I'm sorry, Joe. Don't let her damage what you've got with Fliss.'

'I won't.' Joe tucked Samantha into her car seat. 'Don't worry, Nigel. I'll be able to sort this out just as soon as I get a chance to talk to Fliss.'

CHAPTER NINE

JOE couldn't talk to Fliss.

Her telephone was switched to automatic voice mail. Joe drove straight to Felicity's house but she wasn't there. A note stuck to the front door of the house gave him a moment of hope which was soon dashed. The note was from Felicity's neighbour, Charlie Begg, saying that he had installed the requested rooster in the hen-house that afternoon. Charlie added that he hoped the feathered alarm clock would prove useful and that they would get as many chickens as they wished for. Joe wasn't in any mood to think of future increments to the tribe of hens. He rang the hospital, knowing quite well that Felicity's urgent call had been fictitious—simply an excuse to flee. He couldn't sit waiting for her to come home. Not with a sleepy child in his car. The answering machine requested that a message be left. Joe left message after message.

'We need to talk, Fliss. Call me.'

'Please, Fliss. Let me explain. Call me.'

'Fliss. I love you. *Please*, call me.'

No call came. The silence stretched through a

long, long night. Joe was late for work the next morning, having dropped Samantha at school.

'She's to stay in the after-school care programme until I come back for her,' Joe instructed her teacher quietly. 'If Mrs Jackson comes here, I need to be contacted.'

He went straight to the emergency department on his arrival at Queen Mary Hospital. He spotted Felicity immediately. She was talking to Gareth. She held a lumbar puncture kit in her left hand. A hand that was devoid of a ring.

'I have to talk to you, Fliss.'

'Not now.' Felicity didn't meet his gaze. 'I have an urgent lumbar puncture to do on a two-year-old girl with suspected meningitis.'

'I could do that for you.'

'No, thanks, Gareth.' Felicity declined the offer courteously.

'Yes, please, Gareth.' Joe wasn't going to let Felicity get away with this. He didn't deserve to be treated this way.

Gareth looked from Joe to Felicity and back again. 'It's the third case this week,' he said mildly. 'There's a nasty flu going round that mimics meningitis symptoms.'

'One of them *was* meningitis,' Felicity said defensively. 'We can't afford to treat these cases lightly.'

'I agree.' Gareth nodded. 'But I also agree with Joe. What's going on here is none of my business but it's clearly of some importance. You have to talk to each other so you may as well do it now.' He reached out and took the lumbar puncture kit from Felicity's hand.

'Fine.' Felicity stalked off in the direction of her office. Joe followed, feeling increasingly as though something major was slipping way beyond his control. He had to try and catch it before it was too late. He shut the office door behind him with a decisive click.

'What the hell is going on here, Fliss? Why didn't you answer any of my calls?'

'I wasn't ready to talk to you.' Felicity stood near her desk, her back turned to Joe. 'I'm still not ready to talk to you.'

'Damn it, Fliss.' Joe took hold of her shoulders and turned Felicity to face him. She immediately folded her arms around herself as though experiencing a sudden abdominal pain. Joe kept hold of her shoulders.

'Talk to me,' he commanded. 'What happened last night?'

'You told me to try and see things from Dayna's point of view.' Felicity drew in a long breath. 'I didn't have to try very hard, Joe. She spelt it out for me.'

'Spelt what out exactly?'

'I didn't want to believe any of it.' Felicity's words began to tumble out. 'The pieces wanted to fit together but I made sure I kept jumbling them up so they couldn't connect. I suppose I didn't want to see the whole picture.'

'What picture?' Joe's grip on Felicity's shoulders tightened involuntarily. 'What, in heaven's name, are you *talking* about?'

Felicity pulled free of his hands. 'It might have worked if I hadn't kept remembering things you'd said at odd times. Like wanting to spend time alone with Dayna to tell her about our engagement. It might still have worked if I hadn't seen you kissing Dayna.'

'I didn't kiss Dayna.'

'Don't lie to me, Joe. Not now. I saw you kissing her at the top of the stairs. She wasn't even dressed.'

'You saw *Dayna* kissing *me*. Or trying to.' So that *was* what this was all about. No wonder Felicity was upset. But he could sort it out. He had to.

Felicity's breath came out in a scornful huff. 'Semantics! I knew there was something between the pair of you. The night of that awful dinner party. The way she kept touching you, and looking at you—even the way she talked to you. And how often *does* she talk to you, Joe? More than once a day, by your own admission.'

'OK.' Joe knew he had to be completely honest. 'Dayna thinks she's attracted to me. She always has. That's what I was talking about when I said she'd tried to come between me and Catherine. I thought she'd got over it. I made my lack of any reciprocal feeling very plain at the time. It surfaced again after the holiday in Disneyland last year. She and Nigel had drifted apart and Dayna started writing me letters. That was part of why I had to come back. I had to take my daughter so that she couldn't be used as some sort of incentive by Dayna.'

Joe sighed miserably. 'There is nothing at all between me and Dayna. The only feeling I have for her is gratitude for the help she *and* Nigel have given me with Samantha.'

'I've given you plenty of help in that direction myself, haven't I, Joe?'

'What?' Joe was bewildered now. 'Where did that come from, Fliss?'

'You didn't show any signs of being remotely interested in me the first time we met—at that accident site. You didn't even bother introducing yourself.'

'I was somewhat preoccupied, as you well know.' Joe shook his head. 'This is ridiculous.'

'Is it? I think you got interested after you saw how well I got on with Sam that day in Emergency when I looked after her broken arm.'

'That was the first chance I had to talk to you. I

tried asking you out, if you remember. It was *you* that wasn't interested.'

'I thought you were married. To Dayna.' Felicity smiled with no hint of amusement. 'Silly me.'

'We sorted that out.'

'Indeed we did. We even had a date. If you could call arranging the venue for your daughter's birthday party a date.' It was Felicity's turn to shake her head sadly. 'Was my house and the garden and the animals just a bonus, Joe? Was it more important to find someone who'd be prepared to love Sam? To help look after her now that Dayna was becoming a bit of an inconvenience?'

'I don't believe this.' Joe was staring at Felicity. 'What did Dayna *say* to make you even start thinking like this?'

'She just pointed out what your agenda had been. To find a job and a house and a nanny. You've done well, Joe. Or you must have thought you had. Quite a neat package. And you got to give it a trial run. Maybe I should have noticed when you were so pleased that I offered to help out that week that Dayna went to Australia. You gave me a whole week to prove how well I could fit into your plans. And didn't I do well? It wasn't even a problem for *me* to juggle my roster so *you* wouldn't miss your ward round.'

'Don't do this, Fliss. You're wrong. You are *so* wrong.'

Felicity wasn't going to stop now. Her voice trembled but the words kept rushing out over the top of Joe's. 'Where did you propose to me, Joe? At some romantic venue when we were alone? No. It was in my house with your daughter asleep upstairs. After I'd spent a week trying to prove that you— and I—could have everything.'

Tears weren't far away now. Felicity's voice caught and she cleared her throat. 'Only I wasn't going to have everything, was I? You'd have the career, the child and the lover. I would have ended up having a baby, probably giving up most, if not all, of my career and raising children for someone who doesn't actually want me for myself at all.'

'I thought you loved Sam.'

'I did. I *do*.' A tear rolled down Felicity's cheek. Joe had to resist the urge to pull her into his arms. He had to sort this mess out before he dared touch her.

'Then don't do this to her. *Or* me. Please, Fliss. Listen to me. Sam loves you. I love you. It would break Sam's heart if you—'

'That is an unforgivable thing to do, Joe Petersen.' Felicity's interruption was vehement.

'What is?' Joe's agonised desire to sort things out was giving way to a new feeling. Anger. What could he possibly do in the face of Felicity's stubborn refusal to listen to him?

'To use your own child as a pawn to try and change my mind. It's just what Dayna's been doing to keep a hold on you. Now you're prepared to do the same thing by telling me—'

'Don't you dare tell me I'm using Sam.' The anger was strong enough to taste now. 'I love my daughter. And I love you. I want to be with both of you. I *thought* you felt the same way.'

'I thought I did, too.' Felicity shrugged unhappily. 'Now I don't know what to think. It's a package that's impossible to separate, isn't it, Joe? How could I ever know the truth?'

'You could try believing what I tell you.' Joe's control was slipping. 'For God's sake, Fliss,' he snapped. 'What am I supposed to do to prove my love for you? Give up my job? Refuse to live in a house I haven't bought for you myself? Give up my *child*? Is *that* what you want?'

'No, of course it isn't.'

'Good.' Joe's tone was as icy as Felicity's. 'Because I have no intention of ever doing that again. For anyone. Perhaps what I want or need doesn't really matter a damn. Maybe I was being selfish. It's what Sam needs that should be more important.'

'Of course it should.' Felicity had been avoiding any eye contact with Joe. Now she met his angry stare without flinching. 'Sam needs her father, Joe. And you need a job, a place to live and a nanny. You've got a job now and I'm sure you'll be able to afford a place to live in no time.' Felicity turned away. She picked up an envelope that lay on her desk. An envelope with a lump in it about the size of a ring. She handed it to Joe.

'Try hiring a nanny,' Felicity said quietly. 'It might be more expensive than marrying one but at least it's honest.'

What could he do? What the hell could he do to put this right?

It was an agonising business, even trying to see Felicity's side of this conflict, but it managed to seep in bit by bit as Joe struggled through his day. It wasn't a small issue, asking someone to share the raising of a child that wasn't their own. What if the positions had been reversed and Felicity had the child and needed a job and a place to live? If he was the one who was financially secure with a home ready made for a family? What if someone had suggested to him that perhaps his attractions were such that he might be wanted for something other than just himself? Wouldn't he have had doubts?

Of course he would. It was just so unfair because the doubt was so unjustified. He loved Felicity so much that the thought of losing her was unbearably painful. If their positions were reversed and she had *six* children of her own to raise, he would still want to marry her and provide a home and a future. As long as he knew that she felt the same way about him. With a love that strong they could face anything and make it work. Sharing children, sharing careers…sharing a life. Joe knew his love was strong enough. All he had to do was prove it to Felicity.

But, short of more than a small miracle, how could he do that?

This had to be the worst day of her life. Giving Joe back the ring and ending their relationship had seemed the only possible resolution after last night's agonised analysis of her situation. The feathered alarm clock Charlie had provided had been unnecessary. Felicity hadn't slept a wink. The conversation with Joe this morning had been the hardest Felicity had ever had, but she couldn't risk trusting him any more. The pain might seem unbearable now but how much worse would it have been to go through with a wedding and possibly years of loving a man and his child, weaving her life around them, only to have it ripped apart when she eventually learned the truth? It might be just possible to put the pieces back together at this point. The damage would certainly be irreparable if she allowed it to go any further.

Felicity was grateful that she was the consultant on the trauma team that day. Some challenging injuries might be the only complete distraction possible from this personal crisis. The stabbing victim that came into the emergency department only twenty minutes later provided her first opportunity to test the theory. With considerable relief, Felicity found herself able to focus totally on managing the traumatic chest injury.

'He's got a left-sided haemothorax,' she told the registrar on the team. 'Absent breath sounds and dullness to percussion. We need a large-bore intercostal drain.'

'Do you think there's any cardiac involvement?' Colin was assessing the multiple stab wounds on their patient's chest.

'I think this wound's too low to have done any damage to the heart but we'll get an echo done, stat. These other wounds are quite superficial. He must have put up quite a fight.'

'His hands are a mess.' The house surgeon reinforced Felicity's theory. 'I'll get a new pressure dressing on.'

'See if anyone else is available to help,' Felicity requested. 'We need to get a central line in for rapid infusion. Has someone got the chest drain trolley ready?'

'It's here, Dr Munroe.'

'I need some fresh gloves.' Felicity stripped off and dropped the gloves she was wearing. 'Get his skin prepared and draped,' she instructed the nurse. 'I'll be ready in a second.'

The initial management of the patient's respiratory difficulty was rapid. The ambulance officers who had brought the stabbing victim into hospital were still in the trauma room, completing their paperwork.

'He's got another stab wound,' Felicity heard one report to the house surgeon. 'On his back. Deep laceration at about L4 level. He was complaining of paraesthesia in both feet before his level of consciousness dropped.'

'I'll put in a call to Neurosurgery as well as Echocardiography,' Colin offered.

Felicity tried to ignore the sinking feeling that accompanied the thought of Joe arriving in the emergency department. She nodded tersely and then focused intently on her own task. She had finished infiltrating the skin and periosteum with local anaesthetic. She slid the needle in above the rib and drew back on the syringe. The blood filling the barrel was confirmation that blood was filling the chest cavity on the left side. She made an incision and then used her finger to make a channel for the drainage tube. She was so intent on the procedure she was able to miss Joe's arrival in the trauma room.

'Could we log-roll the patient so I can have a look at his back?'

'Not yet.' Felicity looked at Colin rather than Joe. 'I want to get a central line in and get some more fluids on board. Can I have a head-down tilt, please, and a 12-gauge cannula? I'll go for a subclavian vein.'

It was several minutes before Joe was able to assess the knife wound to the victim's lower back and confirm the need for urgent neurosurgery. Several minutes of his presence that Felicity found enormously difficult to work with. It negated the relief with which she had started caring for this patient and it sent her spirits spiralling downwards even further. There was to be no complete escape from this misery. Not yet. At least it was probably the last time this would happen. Felicity had a day off tomorrow and next week Joe was due to start his locum position at Coronation Hospital. It was highly unlikely he would make regular appearances in this emergency department again. There was only the rest of today to get through.

A late break for morning tea did nothing to help. Colin had brought in a treat for the staff to celebrate his birthday. A piece of the chocolate cake had been

saved for Felicity but she couldn't eat it. She left
the offering in the box the cake had arrived in. A
second glance at the box prompted a wry smile. The
cake had come from a commercial bakery but the
icing didn't look any more professional than her
own last attempt. It looked far too soft. There were
blobs of icing all over the base and sides of the
container.

Felicity had to swallow hard to try and ease the
painful constriction of her throat. For the rest of her
life she knew she would be unable to see chocolate
icing without being reminded of the first time she
and Joe had made love.

Love.

Surely nobody could have made love like that unless they'd meant it? Maybe…just maybe she had
got something terribly wrong. She abandoned any
thought of a break and went back into the department, hoping that it would be busy enough to prevent the inward spiral of her thoughts. The department was certainly busy but the effect of working
hard was not a positive one. Felicity's actions were
purely mechanical. She worked hard, moving from
one patient to the next as quickly as possible, demonstrating clinical competence and maintaining a
professional distance that left no opportunity to find
any joy in her work. Maybe there was simply no joy
to be found anywhere in her life at the moment and

she would just have to accept that. She would look for professional satisfaction instead.

The pager signal that indicated another activation of the trauma team seemed to provide an opportunity for exactly that type of satisfaction. Moving towards the sorting desk, Felicity was able to walk past Joe and still concentrate on her mission. Colin was still finishing the radio transmission to the ambulance service.

'What's your ETA?' he queried.

'Five minutes,' the response came back through some static. 'Do you require any further details?'

'Not unless her condition changes. We'll see you when you get here. Over and out.' Colin was scribbling on a piece of paper as he spoke.

Felicity could hear Joe talking to Gareth behind her as she waited for Colin to finish writing.

'Definitely a cerebrovascular accident. They won't be ready to scan him for thirty minutes, though. I'll come back down.'

'Joe?' A nurse walked past Felicity, carrying a cordless phone. 'Can you take an outside call? They said it was urgent.'

Colin caught Felicity's attention before it could focus on Joe. 'There's been a high-speed car rollover on the Akaroa highway. Thirty-seven-year-old woman. Status 2, coming in by helicopter. Fractured femur and pelvis with major blood loss abdominally.

They've given two litres of saline so far. Systolic blood pressure's down to 85. She's also got chest injuries with a probable pneumothorax but no sign of it tensioning as yet. ETA's five minutes. We'll need…'

But Felicity wasn't listening to Colin any more. The expression on Joe's face as he ended his phone call was frightening.

'Joe? What's the matter?'

'Sam's gone missing. That was someone from her school on the phone.'

'Have they called the police?'

'No. I told them not to. I think I can sort this out myself. I think I know where she is.'

'Where?'

'I think Dayna's taken her.'

'But…' Felicity was confused. Didn't Dayna normally collect Samantha from school? Joe turned away before Felicity could ask any further questions.

'I have to go,' he said. 'I need to find Sam and make sure she's safe.' He started walking towards the doors leading to the ambulance bay.

Felicity had seen the fear in Joe's eyes. For some reason she couldn't understand there was clearly a possibility that Samantha wasn't safe right now. She turned swiftly to Gareth.

'Could you take my place on this trauma team call, please, Gareth?'

'Of course.' Gareth had been watching and listening to the events unfolding around him. 'Go with Joe, Fliss. He needs you.'

'Joe? Wait!' The pause in his stride was long enough for Felicity to catch up. 'I'm coming with you,' she told him.

'You don't have to do that.'

'Yes, I do.' Felicity held the eye contact with Joe. 'I need to know she's safe, too. Maybe almost as much as you do.'

Felicity's love for Joe's daughter was overriding anything else right now. And the love she had for Samantha was inextricably linked with her feelings for the child's father. The three of them were bound together by an undeniably powerful bond. Could Joe understand that?

'I have to come with you, Joe.'

Joe nodded. Of course he understood. 'Come on, then,' he said softly. 'Let's go.'

CHAPTER TEN

THE car park seemed to stretch on for ever.

'How long is it since Dayna took Sam?' Felicity skirted a maroon Range Rover as she negotiated the second row of vehicles. She skipped a step or two trying to catch up with Joe who had his mobile phone against his ear.

'They're not sure.' Joe ended the call he was trying to make and pushed the redial key. 'The teacher noticed she was missing when it was time to pack up for home. The last time she was definitely seen was when they went into the playground for the five-minute break at two o'clock.'

Felicity's glance at her watch was automatic. 'So she could have been missing for an *hour?*'

'The staff are all very upset. They've searched the whole grounds and they want to call the police in.' Joe was covering the ground with determined strides that Felicity was having trouble keeping pace with. 'I've asked them not to—at least not until I've spoken to Dayna.'

Felicity's gaze was fastened on Joe's back but that didn't prevent her noticing the distant shape of an approaching helicopter. The aircraft was presumably bringing the trauma case from the accident on the Akaroa highway—a patient she should have been there to receive. Felicity shook her head slightly, dismissing professional guilt that threatened to undermine her concentration.

'Surely someone must have seen something.'

'Apparently not. All the children have been questioned. I'm sure Dayna's taken her home. It makes sense after last night.' Joe still had the phone to his ear but he was gazing skywards now. The helicopter was getting closer and the noise level increasing.

'Why?' Felicity tried to push back a feeling of panic. Had she contributed to this crisis? Maybe even been its cause?

'Damn it!' Joe snapped his phone back into its holder. 'She's not answering.' He flashed Felicity a quick glance. 'Because I took Sam home with me. I said that was where she belonged and where she would be staying from now on.' Joe had his car keys in his hand. He jammed them into the lock and opened the passenger door first. 'I'd been trying to avoid a direct confrontation with Dayna for Sam's sake. I thought I could find an easier solution.' His gaze caught Felicity's. 'One that would work for us all.' The pain had darkened Joe's eyes so that they appeared almost black. His words were almost drowned by the roar of the helicopter overhead. 'I

guess there are some things there *are* no easy solutions for.'

Joe rounded the front of the car as Felicity
climbed in. She closed her door and reached for her
safety belt. By the time she had clicked it into place
Joe was backing the car from its parking slot.
Felicity waited until the sound of the landing helicopter abated slightly.

'Joe? Put your safety belt on.'

The look Felicity received acknowledged and appreciated her concern for his safety. Joe's lopsided
smile as he complied with the request was enough
to eradicate any final doubts Felicity might have
had. She loved Joe. And she knew that he loved her.
The pain in his eyes when he'd made the comment
about the things there were no easy solutions for had
had little to do with Dayna. Or even Samantha. He
had been referring to herself and the conflict they
had yet to resolve. The pain that was causing him
was so sincere it had cut Felicity to the bone. And
that lopsided smile had been enough to convince her
of the real truth. Joe loved her as much as she loved
him. What did it matter if it had been Samantha's
needs that had brought her and Joe together in the
first place? She loved them. Both of them. And she
needed them as much as they needed her.

This crisis was at least partly her fault. Felicity
had allowed Dayna's poisonous attack to drive her

away from Joe and it had pushed Joe into making a move to protect what he loved. He had taken his daughter and he'd spent the rest of the night leaving voice-mail messages that Felicity had simply erased without listening to. She had to apologise. To tell Joe how much she loved him. But right now wasn't the time. It might distract him from concentrating on his driving as he wove rapidly and skilfully through the lanes of traffic. Felicity didn't want to give any cause for slowing this trip down either. The priority right now was to find Samantha as quickly as possible and make sure she was safe.

The traffic thinned as they approached the Port Hills. Maybe she should say something. Enough to let Joe know that this mission was as important to her as it was to him. That solutions might not be easy to find but they were there, and as far as she and Joe were concerned the solution was not far away. The opportunity to speak vanished as Joe's cellphone rang.

'Yes?' Joe's tone conveyed the expectation of tensely awaited news. The next utterance was one of having heard something unexpected. 'Nigel!'

Felicity could only hear one side of the conversation.

'I have no idea, Nigel... That's what I'm trying to find out... Yes, I know.' A longer pause and then Joe nodded tersely. 'That's what I thought. I'm on

my way to your house now. OK… See you there.'
Joe dropped his phone and increased his speed as
they began to negotiate the steep bends of Cashmere
Road.

'Nigel had a call at work.' The eye contact with
Felicity was brief. 'Dayna was supposed to have collected Scott from school an hour ago to take him to
a music exam. She didn't turn up and they haven't
been able to contact her. Nigel rang Sam's school
to see if she'd been collected and he found out
what's happened.'

'Does *he* think Dayna's taken Sam?'

'He said it was the first thought that occurred to
him. Apparently they had a huge row after I left with
Sam last night.'

'Oh, no.' Felicity's teeth captured her lower lip
with painful pressure. Things were looking worse by
the minute. Perhaps Dayna had kidnapped Sam in
an attempt to get back at Joe and Nigel…maybe
herself as well. She would be well on her way to a
destination that they would have a lot of difficulty
tracing. She might even… 'No, she wouldn't do
that.' Felicity was unaware she had spoken the
thought aloud until she caught Joe's expression.
'Dayna wouldn't hurt Sam, Joe,' she expanded. 'I'm
sure of that.'

Joe looked away. 'Nigel's on his way home. He'll
meet us there. If Dayna's not there he thinks there

might be a clue of some sort. Maybe a note or evidence of packing or something.'

They turned into the driveway of the Jacksons' property only seconds later. The door of the double garage was down. The door and windows of the house were all closed. The atmosphere didn't suggest occupation but Felicity crossed her fingers as she followed Joe to look in the side window of the garage.

Please, let them be here, she prayed silently. *Please.*

'Her car's not here.' Joe turned from the garage and strode towards the front door. He was leaning on the doorbell, creating a continuous ringing, by the time Felicity caught up with him again. He took his hand off the bell and pounded on the door with his fist. The single gesture was an expression of frustration. They both knew that no one was home.

'Hell, Fliss.' Joe leaned his forehead against the heavy wooden door. 'I don't think I can stand this.'

'I know.' Felicity reached up to touch Joe's hair. 'It's going to be all right, Joe. I'm sure of it. And you're not alone. We're going to get through this. We're going to find Sam and she's going to be fine.'

Joe turned and pulled Felicity into his arms. The hug was intense enough to be almost painful.

'You're right,' Joe said gruffly. 'I know you're right. It's just hard to try and keep a grip on this.'

He pressed his lips to Felicity's head. 'Thank God you're here with me, Fliss.'

'I don't want to be anywhere else.' Felicity pulled back just enough to meet Joe's gaze. 'Not ever, Joe.'

The car pulling to an abrupt halt in the driveway prevented the comment Joe seemed about to make. The look that Felicity received and the squeeze on her shoulders before Joe turned to greet Nigel was enough to let her know that the message and implied apology had been understood and accepted. They would talk soon enough. Right now there was something far more important to sort out. Nigel had the key to the house in his hand. They needed to find a clue about where to look for Samantha next.

There was nothing to be found. Samantha's room appeared untouched. Nothing had been removed. There was no evidence that Dayna had planned a trip anywhere. Her clothing and cosmetic supplies were undisturbed. The whole house was as immaculately tidy as ever, apart from the kitchen table. An empty bourbon bottle sat beside an empty crystal tumbler with a rim smeared by crimson lipstick. The tumbler and bottle were surrounded by a snowdrift of damp, crumpled tissues. Felicity was struck by the desolate image of the scene. How long had Dayna been sitting at the table, drinking bourbon and crying?

Joe looked grim. 'When did you last see her, Nigel?'

'This morning. At eight o'clock.'

'How did she seem? What did she say?'

'She was asleep.' Nigel pushed his fingers through his hair roughly and groaned in frustration. 'I didn't like to disturb her. We were up talking most of the night and she was exhausted. I left a note to say I'd be back after I took the boys to school.'

Joe was watching Nigel, listening carefully. 'But you didn't, did you? Come back?'

Nigel shook his head. 'I got a call from the office on my way back. A major crisis had erupted with the take-over of the firm in Australia. I had to go straight in to work to try and sort it out.' Nigel sighed miserably. 'Maybe Dayna was right. She accused me of caring more about my career than her. She said it had been like that ever since the boys were babies. She said she was jealous of Catherine and even more jealous of Fliss. She wanted someone to care about her. To be important to someone. She said Sam was the only person she'd been really important to for years and now you had taken her back so there was no one.'

Fliss was listening as carefully as Joe. There had to be a clue somewhere here. Dayna might have said something that would point them in the next direction to search. Joe's thoughts seemed to be following the same track.

'What else did she say to you, Nigel? Try and remember everything.'

Nigel stared at the tumbler. He reached out and touched the smeared rim. 'She admitted that she had a problem with alcohol. She agreed that she needed help. I thought we were getting somewhere. I told her that I loved her—that she *was* important to me. Terribly important. That the only reason I'd worked so hard for so many years was to give her all the things I thought she wanted.' Nigel's voice caught. 'She said that she didn't care about any of the things we had. She only wanted me.' He looked up at Felicity. 'She was sorry about what she'd said to you, Fliss. She tried to ring you to tell you that none of it was true but you weren't answering your phone.'

'I know. I'm sorry.' Felicity's apology was for Joe as well as Nigel. All those messages that had been ignored. Joe's glance was forgiving but brief. He turned back to Nigel.

'Can you think of where Dayna might have gone, Nigel? Where she might have taken Sam?'

Nigel shook his head. 'Let's try her mobile again,' he suggested wearily. 'If that fails I think we'll have to call the police.'

The level of tension rose noticeably as Nigel

opened his small cellphone and keyed in a number. The ringing began only seconds later and Nigel groaned as they all looked in the direction the sound was coming from. A bright pink cellphone lay on the window-sill above the kitchen sink. Nigel snapped his own phone shut but the ringing appeared to continue briefly, becoming louder. Nigel's perplexed frown cleared rapidly.

'That's the doorbell!' he exclaimed.

Joe and Felicity followed Nigel as he left the kitchen. They stopped on entering the entrance hall when Nigel wrenched the front door open to reveal the presence of two police officers. Felicity's glance towards Joe was startled.

'When did you call the police?'

'I didn't.'

'Neither did I.'

'Maybe the school did.' Joe was trying to listen to the police officer as he spoke.

'Are you Mr Jackson? Nigel Jackson?'

Nigel nodded slowly. 'Yes, I am. What's happened?'

'Are you the next of kin of Mrs Dayna Jackson?'

'Yes. I'm her husband.' Nigel's face drained of colour. 'For God's sake, what's happened? Where's Dayna?'

'I'm sorry to have to tell you this, Mr Jackson,

but your wife's been involved in a motor vehicle accident.'

Nigel's expression was frozen. His mouth opened but he said nothing. Joe took several strides towards the group at the door. 'What about Sam?' he demanded.

The police officer blinked. 'Sam? Who's Sam?'

'My daughter. Samantha. She was in the car with Dayna Jackson. Has she been injured?'

The officer shook his head. 'Mrs Jackson was alone in the car, sir.'

'Are you sure?'

'There were eyewitnesses. It was on the open road. There was nowhere a child could have gone.'

The second officer was staring at Joe. 'Is your daughter missing, sir?'

'She disappeared from school.' Joe flicked a glance at his watch. 'At least an hour and a half ago. We assumed that her aunt had collected her.'

'Mrs Jackson is the child's aunt?' The police officers exchanged a meaningful glance.

Felicity was still absorbing the information the police had given. Open road accidents weren't an everyday occurrence for her emergency department.

'This accident,' she interrupted. 'Was it on the Akaroa highway?'

The police officer raised an eyebrow. 'How did you know that?'

Joe connected immediately. 'The helicopter.' He nodded. 'Dayna was arriving at the hospital as we left.'

'Status 2, thirty-seven-year-old woman.' Felicity remembered Colin's summary of the radio transmission. 'Fractured pelvis, femur and chest injuries.' She turned to Nigel. 'You need to get to the hospital, Nigel. Dayna needs you.'

Nigel was struggling to respond. 'I thought she was dead.'

'She'll be in the emergency department,' Felicity told him. 'She's in good hands, Nigel.'

'We'll take you there, Mr Jackson.'

'Wait a minute.' Joe prevented Nigel's movement to follow the police officers. 'Why would Dayna have been on the road to Akaroa, Nigel?'

'We talked about a place there last night. I'd heard about a kind of retreat for people with problems like alcoholism. I thought they might be able to help. Maybe Dayna decided to go there by herself. Oh, Lord.' Nigel rubbed his forehead with his palm. 'She'd been drinking heavily. Was anybody else hurt in the accident?'

'No. She ran off the road, hit a fence and overturned. There was no one else involved.'

'Thank God for that.'

'What about your daughter, sir?' The police officer turned back to Joe. 'Have you any idea where she might be?'

'I can't think,' Joe muttered. 'I was so sure she was with her aunt.'

'How old is she?'

'Only five.' Felicity supplied the information with a sinking heart.

'Could she have started walking home?'

'No.' Joe shook his head. 'The school's miles away. She never walks home.'

'But she did,' Felicity said. 'When she was staying with me.'

'Does she have any friends from school? Someone she might have gone to play with?'

Joe and Felicity looked at each other.

'Rusty,' Felicity breathed.

'Blackie,' Joe said at the same time.

They both paused and then they both spoke again in unison. 'Sam's gone home.'

Felicity nodded at the police officers. 'Of course she has. It's only five minutes away from school and she knows the way. It has to be where she's gone.'

'She may not be there now.' Joe still looked desperately worried. 'It's a long time since she left school.'

'Let's go and find out.'

The ride across town was as fast as Joe could safely make it. The police officers had scribbled details as

they'd left. A second unit was being despatched as
back-up. If they didn't find Samantha on arrival then
a major search would be instigated immediately.
Felicity had time to make a few telephone calls as
they sped across the city. The school still had staff
available. There would be someone there if
Samantha turned up again. Charlie Begg and his
granddaughter were at home. They were happy to
check the route between school and home and ask
any residents if they had seen Samantha. Her last
call was to the hospital.

'Gareth says that Dayna's OK,' she reported to
Joe. 'Her condition's stable. She needed a chest decompression for a tension pneumothorax and major
fluid replacement after blood loss from the fractures.
She's on her way to Theatre now but he thinks she'll
be fine.'

'She's going to need a lot more than physical repair,' Joe said sadly. 'She's got a big problem.'

'At least she recognises that,' Felicity said gently.
'And Nigel wants to help. I think she'll make it.'

Joe simply nodded. They were turning into
Felicity's driveway now. Dayna Jackson's problems
were part of the future—for the moment their overriding concern was for a child. A small girl with
red-gold curls and freckles who had brought Joe and
Felicity together in the first place and had woven a

bond of love that was now inextricably linked with the love they had for each other.

Joe drove very slowly up the driveway that curved beneath the ancient oak trees, cutting a swath through the lawns. At four o'clock the bright spring sunshine had faded to a warm glow that intensified the colours of the exuberant spring flowers. The gardens were full of the blues of aquilegia and forget-me-nots. The veranda trim across the width of the house mirrored the shade with a froth of wisteria blossom. In the shadows of old fruit trees to one side of the veranda, a fat black pony could be seen dozing contentedly in the afternoon warmth. The house and garden had never looked more beautiful. It was home and it was perfect.

At least, it would be when the people who belonged here were together again. Felicity's confidence that they would find Samantha took a knock as Joe pulled the car to a halt. Rusty always waited for her homecoming at the bottom of the veranda steps. She had been sure he would be in his usual place and that a small girl would be sitting on the steps beside him, patiently sharing the wait. The steps were deserted. The only sign of life was the bees visiting the tubs of pansies in bloom on either side of the bottom step.

Felicity climbed out of the car and whistled. She walked a little way up the driveway and called her dog. Blackie looked up, his ears pricked forward, but the rest of the garden remained undisturbed by any movement. It was unusually still, in fact.

'She has to be here.' Joe's soft tone couldn't hide his despair. 'She *has* to be.'

'She is. I'm sure of it.' Felicity took hold of Joe's hand. 'Look—there are no hens. They only leave the garden if they think someone's going to feed them.'

'She would go to the hen-house.' Joe sounded hopeful now. 'She'd want to look for eggs.'

Holding hands, Joe and Felicity ran through the garden. They slowed down as they approached the hen-house, ignoring the suspicious glare from the rooster who had clearly taken ownership of his new territory. Rusty was also watching their approach from his position lying by the hen-house door. His plumed tail waved a greeting but he wasn't about to move. Felicity caught Joe's glance.

'He's on guard duty.' She smiled. 'And I think I know why.'

The hens inside the coop were clearly waiting to be fed. Their movement and anxious clucking had not been enough to prompt the desired action, however. The potential provider of the food was sound asleep in the corner of the hen-house, curled up in her own nest in the straw, clutching a rather battered white toy dog in her arms. For a few seconds, neither Joe nor Felicity made any move towards the child. They held on to each other, sharing tears of relief and a fierce hug that conveyed a bond they both knew would never be broken. It would never even be questioned. Not again.

The anxious clucking from the hens became more insistent at the continued delay of their meal. The rooster added his grievance by stretching to an impressive height and unleashing an even more impressive crow. The sound was enough to wake Samantha. Large brown eyes opened in the small face.

'Daddy!' The smile was contagious but Joe couldn't quite return it. He was struggling to compose himself as he reached for his daughter.

'Sam! We've been looking for you. You mustn't go away from school by yourself like that.'

'But I came to find Mummy.' Samantha left Woof Woof Snowball in the straw and wrapped her arms around her father's neck as he picked her up. 'You were looking for her last night and you couldn't find her.'

'I've found her now.' Joe was looking over Samantha's shoulder, his gaze locked with that of Felicity. 'And I'm never going to lose her again, I promise.'

'I wasn't by myself, anyway,' Samantha continued brightly. 'Rusty was home. He was waiting for me.'

'He was.' Felicity moved closer at the invitation of Samantha's outstretched arm. 'But next time, sweetheart, wait for me or Daddy to come and get you. It's best if we're all home together.'

'OK.' Samantha was agreeable but then sounded worried. 'I don't have to go back to school now, do I, Daddy?'

Joe's arms were around both Samantha and Felicity. He tightened the hug gently. 'No, Sam. We're not going anywhere. Not right now.'

'Not ever,' Felicity added softly. 'We're home now. Where we all belong.' She kissed Samantha's curls and then looked up to share the joy she knew Joe's gaze would reveal. 'Where we'll always belong.'

'Always,' Joe echoed. His eyes were suspiciously bright and he needed to clear his throat. 'Come on, Sam. Let's feed these hens.'

Samantha shook her head sadly as she looked down at the hens. 'There's no eggs today,' she announced. 'How are we going to get any chickens if there's no eggs?'

'There will be,' Felicity promised. 'Just be patient. There's plenty of time.'

Joe put his daughter down gently and then pulled Felicity close to his side. 'How many chickens can you get in a lifetime?' he asked with a smile.

Felicity's return smile was a little wobbly. 'Lots,'

she said. 'As many as we want.' Her smile widened. 'I think I'd like rather a lot.'

'I don't care how long it takes,' Samantha said firmly. 'I want lots, too. Lots and lots and lots.'

'So do I, Sam.' Joe grinned as he bent to place a tender kiss on Felicity's lips. 'So do I.'

Forrester Square

LEGACIES . LIES . LOVE .

The Kinards, the Richardses and the Webbers were Seattle's Kennedys, living in elegant Forrester Square— until one fateful night tore these families apart.

Now, twenty years later, memories and secrets are about to be revealed…unless one person has their way!

Coming in October 2003…

THE LAST THING SHE NEEDED

by Top Harlequin Temptation® author
Kate Hoffmann

When Dani O'Malley's childhood friend died, she suddenly found herself guardian to three scared, unruly kids—and terribly overwhelmed! If it weren't for Brad Cullen, she'd be lost. The sexy cowboy had a way with the kids…and with her!

Forrester Square…Legacies. Lies. Love.

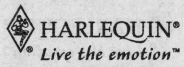

HARLEQUIN®
Live the emotion™

Visit us at www.forrestersquare.com

PHFS3

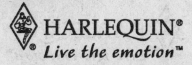

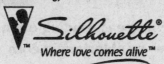

**Treat yourself to some festive
reading this holiday season
with a fun and jolly volume...**

T E M P O R A R Y
Santa

**Two full-length novels
at one remarkable low price!**

Favorite authors

Cathy Gillen
THACKER

Leigh
MICHAELS

**Two sexy heroes find true love at Christmas
in this romantic collection.**

Coming in November 2003—just in time for the holidays!

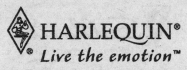

HARLEQUIN®
Live the emotion™

Visit us at www.eHarlequin.com

BR2TS

From Silhouette Books comes
an exciting NEW spin-off to *The Coltons!*

PROTECTING
PEGGY

by award-winning author
Maggie Price

When FBI forensic scientist
Rory Sinclair checks into
Peggy Honeywell's inn late
one night, the sexy bachelor
finds himself smitten with the
single mother. While Rory works
undercover to solve the mystery
at a nearby children's ranch, his
feelings for Peggy grow...but
will his deception shake the
fragile foundation of their
newfound love?

Coming in December 2003.

THE COLTONS
FAMILY. PRIVILEGE. POWER.

Where love comes alive™

Forrester Square
LEGACIES . LIES . LOVE .

The glamour and mystery of this
fascinating NEW 12-book series
continues in November 2003…

RING OF DECEPTION
by favorite Harlequin Presents® author
Sandra Marton

Detective Luke Sloan was hard-edged, intimidating…
and completely out of his element working
undercover in the Forrester Square Day Care!
He was suspicious of single mom Abby Douglas…
but when he realized that her fear was over something—
or *someone*—far more dangerous than himself,
the man in him needed to protect her.

Forrester Square…
Legacies. Lies. Love.

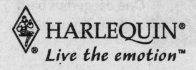